THE SINS OF SEVEN SERIES

RUTHLESS

DANI RENÉ

WARNING

In a world of secrets, where sins are hidden from sight, people live their lives hoping that those around them never know what desires they conceal. The darkest needs, those that taunt just below the surface. Those they hide in the deepest recesses of their minds. Those things they don't admit to. The things they don't talk about. That's what this series touches on. You may find some of the subject matter disturbing, you may even look away, cringe, and gasp. But that's why I wanted to write these seven couples. These couples came to me with their confessions and I obeyed their need to have their stories told. The dark, depraved, the taboo. The things we may find tempting, alluring, and may even be turned on by it. That's what I wanted to write.

Each story is an interconnected standalone, delving into the relationship of the couples you'll meet. There will be sex, there will most certainly be foul language. And there will DEFINITELY be taboo subjects covered.

The Sins of Seven revolves seven couples who are so different in nature, in what their likes and dislikes are. They're each unique in desire, in their personalities, and even in the way they try to show affection. They don't love. At least, they don't think they do, they don't believe they're worthy of it.

Each story will make a point of focusing on one of the seven deadly sins.

Greed, Pride, Lust, Gluttony, Sloth, Wrath, Envy.

Although they'll be released in their own order, you'll be able to tell which sin, follows which couple and their journey to possibly find their happily ever after.

Please heed this warning.

This is a dark romance, suitable for mature audiences, 18+ ONLY. Strong sexual themes and violence, which could trigger emotional distress, are found in this story. Certain scenes are graphic and could be upsetting to some. This story is NOT for everyone. Proceed with caution. Discretion is advised.

"'Tis said that wrath is the last thing

in a man to grow old."

Alcaeus

To the women who've been through hell

and seen the sun rise again.

To those who've needed something more than life offered.

You're strong, you're capable,

don't ever let anyone ever bring you down.

As Madison learns in her story, heal yourself,

nobody else can do it for you.

PROLOGUE

CALLAN

I've never been a good man.

I'm not the man you take home to meet your parents.

Hell, I'm not even the guy you want your friends to meet.

I've done bad things.

So many, in fact, I doubt I'll ever make it to heaven. But that doesn't stop me from living the life I enjoy. If I'm going to hell, I might as well enjoy the ride.

I take each day as it comes. And when I have a job to do, something I've been trained to do, I do it well. I'm a dangerous man. I revel in watching life drain from those whose lives I take.

Six months ago, I moved to Chicago from England,

but my ancestry lies in thick Irish roots. Most people know me as Carrick's older brother. He has a life here; I'm only just starting mine.

Half a year being in another country, and I've taken to it like a fish to water. It's also been six months since I first walked into my brother's club, Seven Sins, and found one alluring beauty who has caught my eye. She's all kinds of wrong for me, far too young and innocent. But that doesn't stop me from wanting her.

Rick has warned me off. Told me to leave her be. Her father is too influential in this city for me to be messing around with her. I've never been one to play by the rules. Hell, I doubt I have any morals left.

I want to listen to my little brother.

But I can't.

It's not because I want to piss him off. It's because this little brunette has lured me into a web of depraved need. She's beautiful, with plump lips that would look incredible around the base of my cock.

Carrick thinks I've already been with her. But I haven't. Apart from in my wettest, wildest dreams. But it's moments like this that turn my body molten — when she walks into Seven Sins every Friday night.

I hear her laughter first, soft, melodic, innocent. Turning to the entrance, I find her along with her friend, Amber Davenport, one of Chicago's elite socialites.

Amber's known for her substance abuse, sexual proclivities, and being better acquainted with the local police officers than her father would like. Which begs the question, why is Madison hanging out with someone like that?

Amber has done well for herself making a name in the media as the bad girl, and she's proud of it. Leggy, blonde, and I'm almost certain a pair of fake tits. But it's not her who's caught my attention. Instead, my gaze lingers on the brunette beside her.

Madison Parker.

Twenty-one-year-old daughter to a senator.

At thirty-seven, I am far too old for her. I should walk away, but like I said, I'm not a good man, so I don't. Instead, I lift an eyebrow as she offers me a small, shy smile. Playing innocent, poppet? I see through her act. Right down to her needy core that she's nowhere near as sweet as she acts.

I know this because of the piercing look she pins me with. Her mouth purses into a pout that causes my dick to leap to attention. And when she lifts her hand to those glossy lips, she bites down on her thumb, and she's hooked me.

The naughty little tease will pay.

I'll make sure of it.

ONE

CALLAN

The club is busy this evening when I enter. Dylan is behind the bar smiling at the men and women he's serving. As one of the longest members of staff, I'm sure he's seen his fair share of things that should be kept secret.

"The usual?" he asks, and I nod, settling myself on one of the high bar stools. My brother is talking to some of the patrons. He's comfortable in this world where men own women, spank and bind them to metal poles for pleasure.

Tonight, I've got a particular submissive meeting me for a special scene. A couple evenings ago, she sidled up to me asking if I wanted to play. I refused but allowed her to leave a number with me, then later messaged her to set up one tonight.

She wanted to talk. That's not something I do. Instead, I told her I'd be here at seven. If she's not here in thirty minutes, I'll find another willing woman to pleasure me. I'm not an affectionate man. I'll fuck you, make you scream, and walk away before you've even come down from the high of your orgasm.

I lean back against the wall, surveying the people moving through the club. The submissives are so easy to spot, the Dominants are like moths to their flames. A gentle melodic sound drags my attention to the corner booth where I spot a familiar brunette.

She's sitting with a friend. They're both leaning in, whispering about something or other. There's a softness to her, rounded cheeks, small button nose, and those fucking curves. I'm about to head in her direction when Celine, my toy for the evening, settles in beside me.

"You're almost late," I offer, lifting my glass toward her.

"I'm here, aren't I?" she quips playfully, but I don't smile. Instead, I pin her with a glare, which causes her to lower her eyes.

18

Dylan sets a glass in front of her, a martini, and her fingers fiddle with the stem, twirling it. She's noticeably nervous when she lifts it to her mouth. Her lips purse along the rim of the crystal, and I watch her swallow almost all of it down.

I love when my prey is nervous; it makes the kill that much sweeter.

She doesn't face me. Instead, she talks to her drink. "What did you have in mind for tonight?"

I lean in toward her, allowing my mouth to hover over the shell of her ear. Lowering my voice, I whisper, "To start, I want to watch you play with your cunt, to make it wet and needy. Using your fingers, you'll open yourself to me. I want to see that sweet, pink flesh pulse before I shove my cock inside you."

A gasp from her lips is all I need to know that she's already wet for me. She's not slapped me, not run away. Instead, she's blushing furiously. The dim lighting does nothing to hide her rosy cheeks.

"Then, we'll play in front of the two-way mirror so all those assholes who love to watch can see how your throat gets fucked so deep you have to concentrate to hold down the puke. And you will, because if you make a mess, you'll lick it the fuck up."

That causes her to snap her gaze to mine, her lips inches from my own. The corners of her lips quirk infinitesimally. "You're vulgar."

"You ain't seen nothing yet, darling," I inform her, rising from my seat. "Finish your drink, take a deep breath, and meet me in the voyeur room when you're ready."

She meets my gaze then. Something dances in those green eyes.

"And if you're not there in ten minutes, I'll leave." I turn and walk toward the back of the club, down the hallway, and toward the room which has cameras set up if someone wants a recorded scene. Otherwise, there's a two-way mirror allowing people on the other side to enjoy the view of the room.

I pull off my black leather jacket, hanging it on the back of the chair. Unbuttoning my shirt, I pull it from the waistband of my jeans and settle myself in the armchair toward the back corner of the room, which allows me to watch the door.

Eight minutes later, it swings open with a soft whoosh, and Celine steps inside. This will be our first scene, but she's confirmed that she's experienced. The fact that she's been with Oliver before tells me she enjoys pain, and I wonder just how far I can take her.

"Get undressed," I order, not moving to go to her, allowing my gaze to rake over her body. She moves slowly, sensually. The red dress she's wearing slips over her slight curves, pooling on the floor, which affords me a view of her in lace lingerie the color of blood—deep, dark, and decadent.

She steps out of the dress on the floor, picks it up, and folds it, placing it neatly on the sofa. When she straightens, her gaze is trained on the floor as she's been taught. Her hands are behind her back, long lithe legs are spread only just.

Perfection.

Silence hangs in the air heavily. Anticipation emanates from her, a perfume of lust and desire. Need and want. She's anxious. Her trembling limbs are a sign she's ready, but she's unsure of my plan.

I enjoy this part of it. The seduction. That unknown

that trickles through you like a poison, covering every inch of a woman's body if I wait long enough. There's no need to rush. Drawing out the experience is so much more intriguing than racing through it. I watch her shift on her feet. It's a slight movement, but I notice everything.

With each silent moment that passes, the anticipation grows. It builds the tension, and I'm hoping her mind is playing out all the scenarios that could happen. If only she knew what was racing through my mind. Some scenes I'd prefer are worse than others.

When her tongue darts out to lick her dry lips, I know it's time to move. I rise, noticing the strain against my zipper. "Kneel," I tell her when I'm at full height.

She lowers herself to the floor. Her hands still behind her back obediently.

"What is your safe word?"

She doesn't have to think about it. "Red."

"Good. Keep your eyes closed and lift your head. Open your mouth." I watch in awe as she obeys. She's beautiful, possibly in her late twenties. I'd say about twenty-eight. I wonder if she's been a submissive for very long. I didn't ask.

Her mouth forms the perfect O. I crouch beside her, making sure the voyeurs can see what I'm doing to her. Taking two fingers, I place them in her mouth, pressing her tongue down.

"Do you know how to suck a cock?"

She nods.

"Swallow it down?"

Again, another ascent.

I lean in, pulling my fingers from between her lips and plant my own over the corner of her mouth. The kiss is sweet, gentle, everything I'm not. I offer her this one get-out clause. One chance to run.

"Are you ready? Because when we start, the only way you're going to get out is if you cry out 'red'."

"I'm ready," she affirms, and I smile.

I rise, pulling my shirt off, placing it on the chair where my jacket hangs. I head to the cabinet and pull out a black blindfold. When I near her, I explain what I'm doing. "A blindfold is the only thing I'll place on you that's soft. The rest will be harsh, painful."

Once it's tied on the back of her head, I move around

in front of her. My zipper hisses as I push it down and pull out my cock.

I trail the tip over her open lips, then shove it into her warmth. The sensation of her throat closing around the tip almost sends me over the edge. But I pull back, then grip her neck, and drive back in, deeper than before. I can feel my dick working into her throat. Her retching and choking only makes me harder.

She doesn't grab at me though. Her hands are still behind her as she convulses over my cock. Saliva drips from her chin, and I'm sure the men watching are already fisting themselves. I continue violating her mouth until I glance down and see the moisture of the tears seeping into the blindfold.

"I love a woman who can take what I have to give," I tell her, my hands on either side of her head. I hold her steady as I slow my pace, reveling in the way her tits shine with the spit dripping over the mounds of flesh.

The scent of her is evident from where I'm standing. So ready for a good fucking. And I'm not known to turn down a woman who's openly wanton.

I pull my slobbered dick out of her and lift her to

her feet. She stands on shaky legs as I shove my wet cock into my pants and tug the zipper up. Reaching for the knife in the sheath, I bring it to her naked shoulder. The cool tip trails its way over the curve, causing her to gasp and recoil.

"If you move, I'll hurt you," I inform her in a low tone. She stills, waiting, her throat working hard as she swallows back the anxiety.

Once again, I allow the steel to tease her skin, slow, meticulous. The thin crimson ribbons of her corset are easily sliced away, and the material falls to the floor. Her breasts are pert, with dark hard nipples.

"Callan—"

"That's not a safe word. Don't make me hurt you," I hiss out, and she shocks the shit out of me by smiling. I take the knife, placing it on her plump lower lip. "This mouth, those lips, they should be silent unless you want to stop."

She shakes her head slowly.

"You realize there are others watching you," I taunt her with a smirk, making her shiver under my scrutiny. "You're wet, darling. I can smell you from here. You're needy for it."

I lean in, running my nose along the curve of her neck, collarbone, down toward her tits. Pulling a dark nub into my mouth, I suck hard, grazing my teeth along the hardened nipple, causing her to cry out in pain.

The sound is like an aphrodisiac.

I follow suit with the other one, pulling and tugging it with a bite so harsh I'm sure there'll be bruises tomorrow.

"You have lovely tits," I tell her. "Speak."

"Thank you."

She's polite, remembering that I told her not to call me Sir, or Master, or any of those fucked-up titles. I'm none of those things. I'm an asshole who gets off on the pain.

I reach up, grabbing a fistful of her hair, tugging her head back so her neck is open for me. My mouth latches on to the smooth, creamy flesh as I suckle on it, biting down hard enough to nip the skin. The metallic taste of blood fills my mouth, and I revel in it like a fucking demon.

Her breaths come fast. I wait for her to cry out her

safe word, but she doesn't. I release her, pushing her to the bed where she stumbles, her hands coming out to save her from toppling all the way over. She lands on the mattress, her body bent at the waist.

"I want to fuck this tight little ass," I tell her, raining down a swat on the globe of her ass.

She yelps loudly, and I offer her another slap, and another. I place one hand on her back, holding her where I want her. Bent over and waiting. With the other, I take my blade and slice away her panties. I know she feels the cold, harsh steel, and I'm certain it's got her scared, ready to run. But once again, she doesn't.

I slide my hands over the cheeks of her ass, opening them to my gaze. From this view, I note her cunt is slick, drenched with need.

I press a thumb on the tight ring of muscle, which has my cock threatening to rip through my jeans. She's fucking tight, and I wonder just how many times she's done this, because from where I'm standing, she looks like a goddamn virgin.

"Reach back, play with your cunt. I want to watch."

She moves her hand between her splayed thighs,

and I can see her two fingers disappear into her sopping hole. The squelching sounds of her juices make my mouth water.

"Finger your ass."

"Callan, I—"

"Are you telling me no?" My voice is harsh, feral. I'm losing all sense of control for this woman who's so tight, so fucking needy for me. "I want to hear you count, while you finger your cunt and that pretty rosebud for me." I don't use my belt because I want to feel her flesh warm under each swat of my hand.

Smack.

"I can't hear you, darling," I taunt.

"One," she whispers in a croaky tone.

Smack.

"Louder," I demand harshly, my voice low and gruff with the word, which causes her to shudder. My palm is stinging and tingling for more, needing to feel her skin give way under my punishment.

"Two." Her count gets louder, but I know by the time she reaches five, she'll be screaming. Her scent is heavy in the air, musky, yet sweet and tantalizing.

"I'm not a nice man. I'll use my belt next. Is that what you want?" My question causes her to shiver. Her head shakes a no, but her quivering cunt is pretty and glistening when I lean in to inhale her.

I lift my hand and rain down another harsh swat on her pale skin. The cock-hardening shade of pink tinging into red appears on her flesh, and I can't help smiling.

"THREE!" she practically screeches, and I grin with satisfaction. The light catches her jewelry when she shifts her fingers, and I note the glint I didn't see earlier. She'd twisted the gold ring around, but since she's been clawing at her supple ass, it's shifted, and the large diamond teases me from her left hand.

She's engaged.

Even fucking better.

I don't pay any mind to the mirror behind me, and I wonder if her fiancé is out there watching his woman be owned by a man who's probably made her feel better than she ever has before. Perhaps he's watching, possibly jerking his dick.

My palm twitches, and I deliver another swat on her ass, reveling in the way the globes jiggle. I've always loved curves on a woman, gripping them while I plough into their bodies. Making sure they remember me for days after I've walked out, leaving them with bruises and bite marks.

"FOUR!"

Smack.

"FIVE!"

My cock is painfully hard, the tip dripping with arousal, and my balls are heavy with need to release inside her. I shove my zipper down, freeing my erection, which is angry. It's throbbing for a taste of her cunt, but before I do drive into her, I slide on the rubber I had stashed in my pocket.

Once I'm sheathed, I nudge her ass with the tip of my dick. With her fingers working both holes, it takes all my fucking restraint not to shoot my load too soon. I wrench her arm away from her ass. Gripping her cheeks, I open them to my hungry glare.

"Please," she pleads into the mattress, and before I have time to admonish her for speaking out of turn, my cock is swallowed into her tight entrance, causing a keening cry to fall into the mattress. She grasps as the sheet beneath with her free hand. The other one still working her pussy as I plough into her ass. Her body is sucking me in, demanding I empty myself, but I don't. Closing my eyes, I focus on the electric current of pleasure shooting through my veins.

I pull out slow and slam back in. My hips smacking against her. The sound loud, echoing along with her moans and whimpers. I won't last long. I know it. I feel the pleasure trickling down my spine as I fuck her. There's no restraint. Nothing more than animalistic pleasure.

"Make yourself come while I own this pretty backside," I order her.

She's close to buckling as my hips meet the cheeks of her ass, faster and harder. Her hips press into the mattress as I grip the flowing strands of black hair, pulling her backward so her face is close enough to meet my mouth.

"Those men are jerking their cocks for you. Do you like that? Is your fiancé sitting there watching you get owned like a little slut?" My words feather over her skin, causing more cries to fall from her mouth. She's so lost in pleasure she can't answer me. There are no words to offer me in response, so I continue fucking her like a man possessed.

I don't know if she's nodding or shaking her head, but I don't give a fuck. All I need is to come. Her cunt tightens, and her tight hole pulses around my cock then tries to push me out, but I don't allow it. I bury myself deep inside her body as my balls draw up, and I empty myself into the rubber.

I move swiftly, pulling out of her once I can think straight. I dispose of the used condom and smirk at the boneless woman on the bed. Righting my boxers and zipper, I grab my shirt and jacket from the chair. Shrugging on the crisp cotton, I don't bother buttoning it up as I head out the door.

With one last glance at her, I offer a smirk.

"Thanks, darling."

TWO

MADISON

My bedroom is bathed in the soft orange glow of sunrise. There's a melody playing through the speakers of my stereo as I stare up at the ceiling. My mind, as always, is on my father's upcoming trip. When he's away for weeks on end, I feel as if I'm alone in the world.

When he's gone, I have to be the face of the Parker household. Sometimes I feel like the princess locked in the tower. Somewhere high above the world so nobody can find me; there's no excitement, merely duty.

Even Hudson, the boy I'm meant to be dating—and yes, I call him that because he's not much older than me—even he doesn't offer me the life I want, and I know he never will. When I think about excitement, I remember the dark-haired stranger in Seven Sins. I don't know him, but when I felt his gaze on me, every part of my body responded.

There was an intensity in his stare that left me breathless. I was almost certain he'd come talk to me, but he never did. He sat at the bar, watching, as if he was the hunter and I was the prey.

He seemed to exude darkness and danger. Something I'd become accustomed to with my father's line of work. Being a senator's daughter puts me in all kinds of situations where I could be hurt, and that's why my father has bodyguards who follow me around as if I'm some sort of celebrity. And I suppose I am in a way.

Which brings me back to Seven Sins, the club I frequent with Amber. It's the safest place in town because of the amount of security. And the anonymity allows me freedom to enjoy a glass of wine without being bombarded by the press.

I started going there a year ago, but since I first saw him six months ago, I've had another reason to go. When I saw him there tonight, I was sitting with Amber, and while she sat giggling about some guy, my eyes were locked on him. I watched as he moved through the crowd. His gaze flitting over to me every few moments. And then I saw him take a woman to the back of the club.

We all know what happens back there. Each room is filled with instruments that can bring pain or pleasure. Since I learned more about it, I've wanted to go back there, to experience it for myself. Perhaps the pain a man like him gives will allow me the release I crave. But for some reason, I've just never had the courage to go into those rooms, to ask a man to dole out pain I know will give me the reprieve I need.

The door to my bedroom flies open, and Hudson saunters in as if he owns the house, this room. He's already dressed in a three-piece suit, and for a twenty-four-year-old guy, he looks far-too distinguished.

Don't get me wrong. I think it's great that he takes care of himself. But I want someone who's rough around the edges. Someone who is almost as uncomfortable in a suit as he is comfortable in black leathers and ripped jeans.

A man.

Dangerous.

And perhaps deadly.

"Madi." Hudson's voice draws me back to the present, to my bedroom.

I scoot up in bed, my brows knitting in confusion. "Where's my dad?"

"He's just left for the office. I thought I'd come up and say hi," he tells me, settling on my bed. His hand reaches out for my leg and rests on my knee, giving it a playful squeeze. The gesture should be sweet, caring, but instead it makes me cringe.

"Won't you be late to the office?"

He shakes his head, his eyes boring into me. "I figured we could get reacquainted." He leans in closer, his mouth on mine in an instant. He dips his tongue between my lips. The kiss, although gentle, is not searing. There's nothing behind it. It's purely mechanical. I allow him to do what he needs as he pushes the blankets aside.

When he moves back to shove my legs apart, I see the wince on his face when he sees them. Those reminders of who I used to be. A teenager struggling with herself. A girl whose mother left her to fend for herself in a world of ruthless politics and a father who doesn't care. When my father told me that she'd died on a cruise ship after having a heart attack, I didn't cry. I didn't feel anything for her.

"We don't have to do this," I tell him, knowing he hates imperfection. He doesn't like seeing what I used to do to myself in the dark of night. No, Hudson wants someone who's flawless. Too bad that's not me. It never will be.

He looks at me like I'm nothing more than a means to an end, and in a way, I am. He settles himself between my thighs without any foreplay. There's no need to get undressed, no need to see more of my flaws. He pulls out his already hard cock and shoves my panties aside. He doesn't touch me. I'm not wet, and when he thrusts inside, it causes me to cry out, not in pleasure, but in searing pain.

He continues to move, sliding in and out of me. And with each thrust, my body slowly responds, growing slick for more, for something other than this cold, mechanical shit we do.

He grunts seconds later, then abruptly pulls out of me, his fist around his cock as he spurts his sticky release all over my thighs. I lie there, angry and unsatisfied as always. Hudson smirks, righting himself as he pulls two tissues from the box on my nightstand.

"That was amazing, baby." He grins. "I have to go. I'll be late." With that, he turns, leaving me to clean up his filth.

Taking the tissues, I wipe myself down, frustrated from the asshole thinking he owns me. My father would be so happy to see us walk down the aisle. But I'll never agree to it. Daddy may rule my life in most respects, but this is something I'll refuse until I breathe my last breath.

Pushing off the bed, I head to the bathroom. I don't want to get ready for the day ahead, but I'll need to if my father flies out this week. There must be a schedule of public appearances waiting for me already.

Sighing, I turn on the shower, stepping under the warming spray. I hope the water can ease the tension in my muscles. I lather up with the orange blossom body wash, inhaling the sweet citrus scent.

The ache between my legs beckons, and I close my eyes, picturing the dark-haired man in his leather jacket. Those piercing eyes that remind me of a midnight sky, which bore deep within me. My fingers move over my clit, teasing and taunting it, and I wonder how his thick, calloused digits would feel as they explored me.

The smirk that curls his lips at times is at the forefront of my mind. Those dirty intentions that ghost along my flesh, his lips, his strong arms. "Oh god," I whimper as an orgasm rakes through me, causing my knees to buckle.

When I open my eyes, I can't help smiling. Somehow, I'll seduce him. Maybe he likes the sweet, innocent look, or even the sultry vixen. I'll find out soon enough.

Mr. Dark and Dangerous, I want you. I want you to show me how illicit you can be.

THREE

CALLAN

"The apartment is perfect," I tell Rick. He doesn't want me to move out, but it's time I find my own space. He's been putting me up along with Cayleigh, our sister, in his guest apartment, which is above Seven Sins.

Carrick owns one of the most elite BDSM clubs in Chicago, along with his friend, Mason. Both men have made a name for themselves, and I'm proud of Rick. I'm older by a year. Not much, but sometimes, I feel so out of touch with everything.

"You're welcome to pay me the rent you're about to give some other asshole, you know." He chuckles, lifting the tumbler to his lips. The amber liquid shimmers in the yellow light. I watch it for a moment, lost in my own thoughts.

"Yeah, but I'd still be living in my baby brother's building," I bite back, but he knows I'm joking. He shakes his head, sighing at my stubbornness. It runs in the family. Perhaps it's an Irish thing.

Even though our roots are firmly in Ireland, we grew up in London. Going back there isn't an option for me, so I've decided to stay in Chicago with my brother and sister. After our little visit to Seamus Moran—the man who killed Cayleigh's fiancé and Rick's fiancée—there's a hit on my head.

Not that I give a fuck. I'll take the assholes down myself, but our father made it clear we're to stay here until he can sort the fuckers out. Of course, I don't mind because I'll be here, in Rick's club where women are abundant and the alcohol flows freely.

"Fine. But, Cal, just watch yourself in the club. I really don't need shit going down." His warning doesn't faze me. I know why he's so wary. I've been known to cause a ruckus at times. But there's a reason I'm dying to go downstairs, and Carrick knows it too.

"You know I'll be on my best behavior, brother." My response earns me a shrewd stare. He's turned into a businessman. In the time I knew my brother, while we worked together, he was one of the only people in our father's organization who didn't enjoy his job.

Working for the Irish mob will do that to a man. You'll end up hating the person you become if you don't embrace it. Carrick never did. Me, on the other hand, I loved it.

"Yeah, I would hope so."

"Come on, Rick. Cut me some slack." I chuckle, landing my gaze on Carrick sitting in his large, black, leather office chair. Fit for a king. Peyton, his submissive is on his lap, twirling his tie with her delicate fingers.

"Fine, you're welcome to play, but don't fucking break hearts. And stay away from Madison Parker," he grumbles. His hands stroke her slim thighs as he watches me with that perceptive glare.

Being older, I've always given him shit, but if there's one thing I can say about Carrick, he's got a good head on his shoulders. The business he started from scratch is booming, and he has a woman who loves him with her every breath. A pretty little blonde who's got curves I wouldn't mind taking for a test drive. Of course, she is my brother's, and I don't do shit like that. Not anymore.

"I don't break anything, unless they ask, Rick," I tell him. I rise from my seat and head to the door. "Oh, and one more thing," I say as I stop at the door. "Congratulations on taking my advice, little brother," I praise him, flicking my gaze over to Peyton.

They were on the outs not so long ago, and I told him to man-up and fight for her. I was in awe at how much she loved him, but when I saw my brother without her, I knew it wouldn't work. He needed her as much as she wanted him. It made sense.

I've never been in love. I don't think it's an emotion worthy of my time. I just don't want it. My kind of work doesn't allow for it. So, I've become accustomed to playing with pretty toys until I have to move on. I told Rick I'd stay in Chicago for a little while longer, but my feet are itchy. I need to make a move.

I leave them in the office and make my way down to the main area of the club. It's not what most people would think. It actually looks like an upmarket restaurant. If you walked in, you'd never guess what delicious delights went on behind closed doors.

The playrooms are off to the right. The bar sits smack-dab against the right wall as you enter the club. And the stage where performances take place is positioned in the center of a circle of booths. You can see it from the bar, but when it's not lit up like it is now, you wouldn't know it's anything out of the ordinary.

If there aren't any shows, most people would think of this as one of those upscale dinner venues, but once the lights are dimmed, there's a sensual undertone that emits itself, and we're met with the decadence of Seven Sins.

Although, most people who frequent it are members, high-flyers — influential people who will pay a pretty penny to keep their names out of the paper for the things they enjoy doing behind closed doors. I mean . . . who wants a congressman to be into kink?

Being within the walls of this place makes me want to take a slave and mark her. I want to play, but what my brother doesn't realize is that as much as he wants to confine me to a certain mold, I won't remain in that box for very long.

I'm far from what most of the men here are. No,

44

I don't have a specific kink. Unless you count the obsession I have with a certain brunette. If only I could see her pretty porcelain flesh against my sleek, silver blade, I'd die a happy man.

Morality isn't my strong suit.

I do things because I can.

When a woman relinquishes everything to me, my restraint disappears. The beast that resides within me awakens, and its hunger knows no bounds. Nothing is sacred.

I've had my fair share of experiences, but I'm different than Rick. He's a Dominant who can love with gentle touches and kind words. I'm far more sadistic than he is. I need a woman's full and ultimate submission. Her body is mine to toy with, to abuse as I wish, but I don't just take, I give a lot too. She'll experience pleasure she never knew existed. All by my hand.

Settling at the bar, I ensure I'm facing the booth where my newest pet is sitting with her friend, Amber. Two other girls have arrived who don't look at all familiar.

I turn to find Dylan wiping down the bar top. He

glances up at me. "Can I get you a Jameson?"

"Yeah, can you make sure it's a three-finger shot? I think I'm here for the night."

He nods, moving along the bar to get my drink. My brother didn't keep Irish whiskey in the bar when I arrived, but over the months of me spending my time here, he's assured there's always a bottle behind the bar for me. While Dylan is away, I turn my attention back to Madison. Her dress has ridden up her lithe legs. The sparkly orange material shimmers under the lights of the club.

"She's a beaut," Dylan says, setting the tumbler on a coaster in front of me. "Too bad her boyfriend is such a prick."

I snap my gaze to his. "Boyfriend?" My brows furrow in confusion as shock settles at the realization I know nothing about her personal life. Let alone her professional one. All I know is she's Senator Parker's daughter.

"Yeah, he's her dad's right-hand man," Dylan intones with a hint of sarcasm on the "right-hand", which makes me wonder what he knows that I don't.

46

"A twenty-four-year-old prep-school boy," he continues with frustration evident in his voice. Jealousy. I should laugh, but I feel it too.

"So why is she in here if she has a boyfriend?" I question, lifting the drink to my lips.

"Dunno. She's here every Friday with her friend. I think he's away or works late. She never stays after midnight, though. Perhaps she's like Cinderella." He chuckles, leaving me to mull over the information he's just offered.

The whiskey burns its way down my throat in a fiery blaze. I don't turn away from her, intoxicated just by the sight of her curves in that barely there scrap of silk she thinks is a dress. Which makes me wonder what her panties look like. Madison's gaze darts to mine as if she can feel the heat of my penetrating stare.

Those pretty, cinnamon-colored eyes that linger a moment too long tell me she wants this. Me. And I've never been able to say no to a woman who begs. She may not use words, but she definitely tells me with the soft, sweet smile that lifts her full, rosy lips she's ready for the predator inside me to devour her beautiful, silken skin.

Turning to Dylan, I lift my empty tumbler.

"Tell me something," I start. "Does she ever go into the back rooms?"

"Nah, never seen her back there," he tells me, then shakes his head. "Actually, there was once I saw her watching a scene. Oliver Michaelson had taken a pretty sub into the viewing room. There was a lot of talk about how he'd used her. I saw bits here and there. It was hot. But Madison's never been with a man back there."

"Thanks." I rise, tapping the bar.

"Not having another one?" he questions, raising the empty glass.

Shaking my head, I respond with my new apartment in mind. "No, I have some place to be." I make my way toward the exit, purposely passing her table. Once out on the street, I zip up the leather jacket I'm wearing. It's chilly out tonight, but as spring nears, I know it will warm up soon.

"Hey," a soft melodic voice calls to me. When I spin on my heel, I find her standing there in her pretty little dress. "Leaving so soon?" She sidles up to me, her hips swaying as if she's ready for what I want to give her. But she's so far from ready. Her body is the perfect curve of an hourglass. Narrow waist with wide hips. Her tits are more than a handful, and I know they'd look perfect with my dick between them.

"Yeah, places to be, people to see," I offer, picking up the helmet from my bike. I hate driving, so riding is my choice. The Ducati Panigale V4 is my prized possession since I moved here. Bright orange, like Madison's dress, it's one of the most beautiful bikes I've ever owned. The power is incredible, the speed is out of this world, and all I can think of is having her sitting behind me, holding on as I race down the highway.

"A girlfriend?" she questions, lifting one dark, sculpted eyebrow in question. Her skin has a soft glow from the outside lights, making her seem almost ethereal. I say almost, because there's nothing angelic about the way she's currently looking at me.

"No. I don't do girlfriends."

She smiles at my response, and I wonder why. If she has a boyfriend, shouldn't she be with him right now? Instead of standing in a parking lot talking to a man who can and will break her?

"I'd like a ride sometime." She gestures with her chin at the bike behind me.

I glance back, mainly to hide my smirk. Dragging my gaze back to her, I watch as she nears me in her black fuck-me heels, closing the distance between us even more. We're merely inches apart. Her body shivers, trailing over her frame, and I wonder if it's from the chill in the weather, or if I'm affecting her as much as she is me.

"Oh?" Lifting my brow, I wonder if daddy knows she's dressed like a little harlot asking for a fuck. And I wonder if she takes it like one too. I'd love to find out. My cock is thick and throbbing in my jeans. It's ready to be let out, to drive into her and tear her in two.

"Yeah," she quips, folding her arms across her perky chest, which only serves to push her tits up. My tongue darts out, licking my lips as my eyes drink her in slowly.

She's nothing like the fine wine I pegged her for.

No, this girl is a smoky, spicy bourbon.

"I don't play with little girls," I growl, leaning in closer to inhale her scent. Sweet, innocent, and so damn dangerous. One taste and I know I'll be hooked. My body is tense. Holding onto restraint while so close to her is difficult.

She raises her head, meeting my intense gaze. "I'm not a little girl," she bites back, causing me to chuckle.

I take a step toward her, causing her to shuffle back. I don't stop until she's pressed against some rich asshole's Ferrari. I run my nose over her cheek, reveling in the perfume that reminds me of sweet citrus. "You're very little, sweet thing." I allow my words to feather over her flesh, earning me a tremble. "And a man like me could break you."

I wait for her to run back inside, but she doesn't. Instead, she stays in place, still, unmoving, until I lift my hand and trace it along her bare arm. Smooth, silky skin dots with goosebumps at my touch.

Jesus, this woman is far too beautiful for me to violate. There are so many filthy, sinful things I'd love to do to her.

"I don't break easily," she informs me, an infliction of need in her voice. It's a gentle tug at my cock, as if she's trying to jerk me off with her words.

"Be careful what you wish for, Madison Parker, because you might just get it." I reach for her ass, my big, calloused hand gripping the globe of flesh, squeezing hard until I get the whimper I've been aching to hear. And it's perfection.

"Why don't you give me your number?" she asks.

I step back, my hand lowering to her hip, holding her in place in case she decides to run away. "Why don't you give me your phone, sweetheart?" I coax.

She doesn't think twice about handing me her mobile. I punch my number in, send a quick message to myself, then lock the screen once more. I haven't saved it because I plan to toy with my food before I eat it.

"Keep it on you tonight when you go to bed. And ensure that pussy of a boyfriend isn't around." I turn and saunter to my bike.

"He's not my boyfriend," she calls to me.

I don't respond. Pulling on my helmet, I swing my leg over the bike and start the engine. A loud, snarling roar. The vibration between my legs, the power of the machine, and the pretty brunette who has my number have my cock ready to explode.

FOUR

MADISON

I watch the motorcycle fly down the road, my body still reeling from being so close to him. It's not the first time I'd seen him here, but it was the first time I spoke to him. The dark stubble on his jaw, the ripped jeans, and tattered leather jacket make him look rough, dangerous. But it's his smoky growl that makes my knees wobble.

I wonder what he'd think of me if he really knew me. Sadness threatens to consume me, but I push it back down. I've been in the public eye for too long, and having someone like him in my life would never work, but perhaps he could be my secret. Mine alone to enjoy in the dark.

Dad would have a fit if he knew where I was. So would Hudson. My so-called boyfriend. All the fake smiles and lies I have to bear because of my father's job have left me rebelling. I come here every Friday, when I can get away from their watchful eyes, to enjoy myself.

I may not be a submissive by any means. But my needs do tend to gravitate in the murky waters of dangerous desires. And it seems the dark stranger with the piercing midnight eyes may just be able to give me what I need.

Each day, I wish I could be normal. Just another twenty-one-year-old girl who doesn't have to be careful what she wants in case her father loses his job or gets bad press for something she's inadvertently done.

I'll never be perfect.

I just want my father to accept that.

Turning on my heel, I make my way back into the club. Once I'm seated with my friends, I can't help my smile faltering when Amber questions, "What did he say?"

"I didn't catch him. He was gone by the time I got out there," I respond with my fib. She doesn't pick up on it because I've been taught by my father to lie. For years, I've smiled, put on a show for everyone who was watching. *Family first, Mads,* Daddy would say, even though he wouldn't know the first thing about love and affection and putting those you care about first.

Sighing, I lift the wine to my lips, savoring every drop like it's my last. For the next two weeks, I'll be lazing around the house, if I'm not out at meetings with various charities. I wish my father would allow me to work at the office, but he's got it in his head I need to be at home, looking after the house. He's an old-fashioned man, believing women should be in the kitchen, pregnant and barefoot.

Since I turned eighteen, he's become more adamant that I'm supposed to learn how a woman runs a house. However, being in charge of our staff complement doesn't fill me with excitement. They cook and clean, ensure the place is spotless, even though there are only two of us who live in the goddamn house.

My mother used to stay as far away from the house as possible. When she ran off with one of the men who worked for my father, I was angry. The fact that she was screwing around on my father was well-known by the people who clean our home. I overheard them talking about it, but I never said a word. Instead, I used to spend my time in my bedroom, where no one can judge me for my own indiscretions.

When I heard she'd died, I didn't feel a thing. I was numb to any emotion I had for her. The last time I'd seen her, she told me I would have a better life with my father. If only she knew.

"Earth to Madi." Amber giggles, waving her hand in front of my face. "Where did you disappear to? That hottie really got to you, didn't he?" she questions, smiling at me with those big eyes.

There are times I feel far removed from my best friend. I think she'd be better off being the daughter of a senator rather than me. I don't fit into their world.

"No, it's just been a long day. I think I'm going to head home," I tell her. Another lie. Just stacking them in the corner for later. Rising from the seat, I offer them a smile. Amber is one of my best friends, but right now, all I want to do is be alone. Or with him. But he left, and my heart hasn't yet calmed to its normal pace.

"I'm going to talk to one of the hotties at the bar," Amber informs me. She's a party animal, and I'm the quiet one. Even though my dad doesn't know half the stuff that happens when I'm out with her, he seems to like Amber.

"Have fun, babe. I'm just not feeling it tonight."

She rises, giving me a hug. "Don't be a stranger. I need you tomorrow for our shopping date," she tells me excitedly.

"I'll be there," I promise, but somehow, I don't think I'll make it. My mind is still a mess from the man with the intense indigo eyes. His dangerous aura only seemed to make me want to learn more. My heart hadn't sped so fast in a long while. Since I was a teenager with a crush. Now an adult, I want that feeling.

Tomorrow, I'll ask one of my father's investigators to find him. It can't be too difficult. I have a photo of him on my phone, which I took sneakily one night as he'd sauntered in here. Heading toward the exit, I find my driver sitting near the door.

"I'm ready," I tell him.

He nods, rises, and leads me out to the Town Car that's chauffeured me all my life. Growing up with money afforded me privileges, but all those don't compare to the one thing I do want. To be a normal girl who's able to lose control just once. My life has been filled with rules, regulations, and I've been followed around by bodyguards ever since I can remember. Perhaps that's what the stranger did to me. He gave me a glimpse of that danger I've always looked for.

That trickle of excitement that causes butterflies to attack me with vengeance. To heat my blood and leave me restless at night when I'm alone in bed. My body burns for it. It aches so deep within me I feel it in my soul. I want that searing heat of a man's touch. His gaze boring into me as if he's trying to rip me apart.

I want passion.

For him to unleash his wrath on me.

As much as I love Amber, shopping for the latest Dior or Versace isn't on my ultimate to-do list. No, I need him.

The car weaves through the darkened streets as I take in the city lights. There's something magical about a city. It's alive even in the dark. It calls to the heart of you, begging for you to enjoy what secrets it hides.

Moments later, the car stills. "We're here, Ms.

Parker," Ronald tells me, and I realize I'd been lost in my own head once more.

"Thank you, Ronnie." I smile, exiting the car. He hates when I call him that. But when someone has known you your whole life, they make exceptions for your inadequacies. Making my way up to the door, I unlock and shove it open to find the lamps leading down the hall to the kitchen glowing with the faint yellow bulbs. Those are the only lights on, and I recall Daddy telling me he'd be home late from the function tonight.

Sighing, I drop my keys in the bowl at the entrance and head up the stairs to my bedroom. The space has been my own all my life. A place where I can be myself. The black curtains, orange throw cushions, along with soft gray walls and the off-white carpet make it palatable. The rest of the house is filled with my mother's taste in furnishings.

I have a king-sized bed against one wall, windows which overlook the back gardens toward the left of my bed where I can see the moon on a clear night just beside it, a walk-in closet with more space than I know what to do with, and a private bathroom attached.

Pulling off my shoes, I revel in the soft cushion of the carpet. Thick and warm against my sore feet. I hate wearing heels, but going to Seven Sins means I have to dress up. I enjoy the elegance of the club rather than wearing next to nothing and heading out to the seedy places Amber prefers at times.

What I want is something vastly different. I need to be taken. Harsh and rough, made to feel. Since I turned thirteen, I knew I wasn't like other girls. Being different caused me to get bullied every day. I never had friends. I didn't go to house parties like the rest of the kids did. I was teased my whole school life. The bigger girl with the braces. Even now, when I think back, it hurts. Nobody realizes just how much words can damage.

Nobody would recognize me if they saw me right now. I was always curvy. Bigger than the rest of the petite girls who could wear anything on the racks. I would hide behind floppy sweaters and loose-fitting tees. But that's not the only reason I hid.

Blinking the tears away, I flop onto my bed and stare up at the ceiling. When I'm overwhelmed, the sadness resurfaces. It slams into me, reminding me I'm human.

We can hurt. We can bruise so easily. It's those scars I hide beneath the expensive dresses I wear.

I pull open my drawer and find my journal waiting for me. It's been years since I owned my first one. Writing my thoughts have helped, but sometimes I need more. I want the pain to leave my body one way or another.

Even though I know a scene might satiate the craving I have, there's never been someone I trusted enough to accept an offer.

Not even Hudson has ever once given me what I crave so much. When I asked him to spank me, he blanched at the thought. And even with him, there isn't heat or desire.

He's been the only man I've been with other than my epic failure of a first time. It was a fumbled mess that left me wanting. I gave up my virginity to a boy in school because I wanted to feel something. The pain. The sting of his dick sliding into me. Breaking me made me feel alive.

It wasn't good.

There was no emotion.

When Hudson had come into the picture, I was

almost happy. It was a reprieve for me to finally have someone who wanted me. Until he learned about my secret, he did want me. And with him, I allowed myself to forget the years of bullying and torment. I even shoved those angry words and sneers directed at me into a little box. But no matter how much time I spent with Hudson, he never offered me solace because as soon as he was gone, I'd reach for the razor.

The moment I turned thirteen, I told my father I wanted to go to defense classes. He didn't understand why, but I explained that if one of the guards wasn't around, at least I'd be able to defend myself. Finally, after more begging on my side, he agreed. I know how to fight, to take a man down. I'm stronger than I was before, and slowly, I've become more comfortable in my own skin.

I pick up my stereo remote and turn on the song I listen to when I'm in this mood. "Numb" by Linkin Park screams through the speakers as I bleed words onto the page. It's an old diary with yellowing pages that allows me to express myself with words when I have no one else to talk to.

My phone vibrates on the nightstand, startling me. When I pick it up, I notice a number I don't recognize. Swiping the screen, I lift it to my ear. "Hello?"

"You alone, sweetheart?" The gruff tone of the stranger from the club sounds through the speaker and somehow travels through me, igniting heat in every inch of my body.

"I am." My confirmation earns me a grunt from the other end of the line, and I wonder what he's doing. Is he alone? Is he on his bed or sofa? "I didn't think I'd hear from you."

"I don't play with little girls, but you've intrigued me, baby," he murmurs. The word *baby* in his thick Irish accent only serves to send me spiraling with need. My core pulses, and I'm tempted to touch myself while he speaks.

"I'm not a—"

"Yeah, I know. You're not a little girl. Tell me something. Why me?" He sounds genuinely curious. I lie back on the mountain of pillows adorning my bed and listen to him.

"You're dangerous."

"I am," he concedes easily, and I know I've made the right choice. "And that's all the more reason for you to stay away from me." It's a warning. One I won't listen to. I've never been good with authority. Unless it's my father who seems to force shit on me. Shit like Hudson, who thinks he's got a claim to me. I know the only reason he's near me is because my father hired him to work in the senate office.

"What if I want the danger?"

"I'm no good for pretty young girls." Once more, his warning falls on deaf ears. "Are those pretty panties wet right now?" His gruff question sends a heated tingle trickling over my skin causing goosebumps to rise everywhere.

"They are," I tell him honestly. I may look like a sweet, innocent girl, but you should never judge a book by its cover.

"Then touch them. I want to hear you," he orders in a husky tone. My fingers trail down between my legs. My pen and journal forgotten when I reach my pussy. The material is slowly getting wetter with each word he utters.

A moan falls from my lips unbidden, but I earn myself a husky growl in response.

"Slip them to the side. Imagine my finger stroking you. Are you shaven, Blossom?" he inquires easily.

"I'm smooth. Warm. Wet." My words elicit more sounds from him I'm certain is him jerking himself off while listening to me. "Are you . . .?"

"I'm fisting my cock. It's hard because of you and that hot fucking body." He grumbles once more, and I can't stop the smile on my face.

"You're a pervert," I retort, but I'm sure he can hear my smile. My fingers still teasing my clit, finding myself so wet I'm sure he can hear the sounds of my ministrations.

"And that's why you want me." He's right. He's filthy and dangerous, and perhaps even a little depraved. "Did you want my cock in your cunt in that parking lot, sweet thing?" His filthy words are feral. A need we both feel overtakes us, and I whimper as his moans rumble over the line. "That's it, come hard for your filthy fucking pervert on the phone."

My body shudders and shakes as an orgasm rips

through me. My toes curl into the sheets; my body bows off the bed as pleasure zings over my skin, rippling like a wave crashing on the shore. Trickling into nothing.

"You're beautiful, Madison Parker," he murmurs as I come down from a high I've never before experienced. I've been with a man before, fucked and touched myself, but nothing compares to what just happened, and he hasn't laid a finger on me yet.

"You don't know me," I respond, breathless and wanton. This can't be a one-time thing. I want this man to obliterate everything that's hurting me. I need him to take the ache inside me away.

"And you don't know me either," he tells me easily, and he's right. I don't know him, but I want to.

"Why don't you come and steal me away?" I question. "Tomorrow. Come see me. Give me a ride on your motorcycle," I urge him.

"Madison." He breathes my name in his thick accent, which doesn't help ease the yearning for him. "You're playing with fire." The man has warned me off him so many times in this conversation, but I haven't yet given up. I don't want to.

"I like to get burned." My words earn me another grunt. "Please, Pervert, burn me." My plea is breathless, filled with wonder and hunger. I'm starving for it.

"Callan," he says.

"What?"

"My name is Callan. If you call me pervert one more time, I'll come over there right now and spank your ass red-raw, then I'll fuck it until you're a bloody mess on my shaft."

I can't stop the whimper that falls from my lips at his filthy promise. A vow to hurt me. My body responds with a tremble. My legs splay wide, and I spank my own mound so hard I cry out in the darkness.

"Do you like that, Blossom? Me making you hurt and bleed?"

"Yes."

One word is all he needed to curse a growled *Jesus Christ* down the line.

"You're a very bad girl, Madison," he admonishes me, but there's a tell in his tone. A feral rumble of desire I know I've caused. He wants me as much as I do him.

"That means you'll have to punish me," I say,

smiling as he goes silent, and I wonder what's running through his mind right now.

"Tomorrow, you'll be at Seven Sins at eight, where you'll wait for me until I arrive. I have shit to do during the day, but if you really want this, then you'll be there. Am I understood?" he commands easily, and something tells me this man is used to getting his own way. "And wear a dress. I want those legs bare for me."

"What makes you think I'll even be there?"

"You will. Because you know that your prep-school boyfriend can't make your pretty pussy wet like I can. And you're the one who sought me out, sweetheart. Don't forget, if you're not at the club tomorrow night, I'll walk away, and you'll never see me again." He's adamant. I nod to no one. He can't see me, and how I wish he could. Because he'd see how needy I really am for him.

"Till tomorrow."

He doesn't respond as the line dies. The ceiling dances with shadows as the moonlight shines through the windows. My face cracks into a big smile. Excitement tickles my stomach like a million butterfly wings flapping wildly.

He's right about so many things. It's dangerous meeting a man I don't know, but it's in a public place. At least, that's what I tell myself as I head into my bathroom to get ready for bed.

I brush my teeth, taking in my flushed reflection in the mirror. The orgasm he gave me was amazing, but slowly doubt seeps into my mind. I try to shove it away as it attacks me. I can't though, because if he sees me naked, he'll know.

Perhaps we can do whatever he has planned without needing to get naked. He wanted me to wear a dress. He can easily lift it up without taking it off. Nodding, I decide that's the easiest way. As the thought lingers in my mind, I realize I've already decided I'll fuck him. I want to.

With that thought weighing heavily on me, I slip under the covers and close my eyes, hoping my mind will ease up and sleep will steal me.

FIVE

CALLAN

Pulling the knife from my glove box, I run it along the dashboard, watching the blonde woman kiss the asshole. Only she's no woman, she's a girl. Oh, the lies that riddle this man's life are like a venom slowly trickling through every pore on his body. His hands cup her pert ass cheeks, gripping them as he lifts her. They move into the bedroom, and my gaze trails along with them. It's light enough to see her body straddle his, and my cock rages behind my metal zipper with images of Madison Parker riding me just like that.

After my earlier phone call with the feisty little tease, I'm still hard as fuck. Solid steel, painful and throbbing for her tight cunt. The sounds of her finding pleasure while talking to me were more than I could take as I let spurt after spurt of hot release streak my bare stomach.

A soft vibration sounds beside me, and I wonder if it's her, but then I remember I was expecting a call. "Oliver," I answer after glancing at his name flashing on the screen.

"How are you doing, O'Leary?" he questions, and I can hear the smirk in his voice. He's one of Carrick's contacts, a man everyone wants to know, and every person who visits Seven Sins wants to fuck.

"The usual," I respond. "I've been watching them. It's definitely the blonde from Sins. No doubt Mr. Parker is deep in this, and there's no way he's getting out. I wonder if she has a magic pussy or something?" I can't help chuckling.

He sighs at my observation. "That is interesting. She's going to be named along with him in this. I wonder just what she wants from a man like that. He's old enough to be her father," he says. Once again, there's a confidence in his tone. The man exudes it like a goddamn cologne.

My eyes are glued to the scene before me. The

man leans in. His mouth finds her nipple, and her back arches. My hand moves instinctively over the bulge in my jeans, squeezing, gripping my cock as he pulls her panties down those long, lithe legs. She smiles up at him. There's nothing sweet about her, it's all sinful, vile, and I know that this woman is a threat to Madison in more wats than I ever could've imagined. And Magnus seems to be playing the *innocent daddy* role far too well.

"Oh, she's giving him the ride of his life. Even though she's half his fucking age," I grunt out in frustration. Madison is pretty much half my age, but I still want her on her knees swallowing my dick, looking up at me with those pretty eyes. Is it wrong? Perhaps. But I don't care.

"Let me know when you can send the footage, and I'll make sure it's edited so her father will see just how his precious daughter is spending her time. Also, I've set up an interview for you tomorrow. Mr. Parker needs someone to assist while he's away. He leaves on Friday. His daughter needs a bodyguard of sorts."

This perks me up. "Oh?"

"Yeah, and you'll have access to his house. I'm

sure you can find a way into his home office where he has all the documents we may need."

"Sounds good. I'll be there."

"Make sure you land this job. It's our only way into the Parker house," he warns, but he doesn't need to tell me that.

"Do you really think that low of me?" I question, chuckling. "I'll land it. He'll be begging me to work for him." I stare out at the skyline twinkling beneath the dark sky. The possibility of playing with little Madison causes me to harden fully.

"Be careful of the daughter. She may be beautiful, but she could be as bad as her father," he tells me as if he's reading my mind.

"Well then, she's just met her downfall, because I'll break her until there's nothing left." It's a promise, my voice steady with the threat hanging heavily in it.

"If you need anything, call me."

"Thank you, Oliver."

He hangs up without responding, and my phone beeps with incoming mail. A smile tilts my mouth. Magnus Parker is taking what he doesn't deserve. Things that shouldn't be done when you're in his position of power, and that only makes me want to hurt him more. To see him bleed. And the one way I know I can easily do that is through the pretty brunette. Madison will be easy pickings. Magnus will feel wrath, not only mine, but that of the public he's put on a show for all this time.

My eyes are glued to the erotic scene before me as he shoves his boxers down. My blade glints as I move it toward my mouth, my tongue darting out as I lick the sharp edge, palming my cock as he drives into her. He's gentle, loving, and sweet. So far from who I am, what I hunger to do to women.

They move in sync, their hips coming together. They're connected. They're making love at a pace that would be construed as affectionate. But he's a liar; he's a vile creature. And I know for a fact that the filth he hides will soon be brought to the surface.

I may not kill him, because torturing him may be even more satisfying. I'll break his daughter down to nothing. He'll watch me use her until there's nothing left. Revenge is easy. All you need is a cold, dead heart, and I have one of those. Oliver's earlier warning about her only has me ready to really see what she can handle. If she's as feisty as I believe, I can't wait to see how she crumbles beneath me. It doesn't hurt to have some fun when you're on a job.

I enjoy a challenge, and I have a feeling the little curvaceous brunette will offer me just that. After her whimpering on the phone earlier, I know one thing for sure. Madison is a needy little girl who loves it rough. She certainly did enjoy the filthy words I spewed.

The precious little girl wants a ruthless killer instead of a clean-cut politician. Her little cunt will drip when she's blindfolded, bound, and flogged. I'll ensure her body trembles with need when I show her just how far I'll push her outside of her boundaries. The more risqué, the better. And soon, I'll give her exactly what she desires.

They move faster, and so does my hand. I'm jerking off, watching a woman fuck the asshole who I want to drain of blood. The sickness that lies in my mind as my eyes stay glued to them turns me on. It makes me hunger more, so much more. I watch her come. She bows off the bed; her body shudders, but it's not real.

If there's one thing I've learned about women, it's that they're brilliant actresses. They may come across as innocent, not showing off that need that's hidden deep in the recesses of their minds, but it's there. Hidden, because they know that society will shame them for wanting it. It takes a real man to draw it out. A woman can play any man with a pout of her full, red lips.

They finish, and when I glance down, I realize I've spurted sticky semen all over my hand. Dropping the knife on the seat beside me, I grab tissues and clean myself. Once I'm done, my attention is once again on the house before me.

The lights are out. I know they're asleep because this is the fifth night in a row I've been here. I've watched them make love, him inside her. But every single night, she's put on a show to ensure his ego is still fully inflated, and I wonder just how much he's paying her.

Sighing, I lean back on the leather seat, reveling in the thought of finishing this job. When I finally watch Mr. Parker take his last breath. I stop the camera from filming and slide it into the small black bag. The footage is all we'll need to ensure Mr. Parker plays nice.

Starting the engine, I pull away from the house. I'm tempted to go to her. The house may be secure to her father's standards, but I know where the weak spots are in his security system. I can easily slip through her window and steal her before she even realizes what's going on.

The thing she doesn't realize is that as soon as she approached me outside Seven Sins, she became my prey; and soon, when I unleash the hunter she so clearly forgot about, she'll rue the day she ever begged me to take her.

As I weave through traffic, I take in the skyline. Chicago is beautiful at night. Any city has a shimmering beauty in the darkness. I revel in it. In the shadows. My life has never been easy. Growing up the son of a mobster wasn't all sunshine and rainbows. I've seen death, I've tasted blood, and perhaps that's why I've become the way I am.

When Carrick told me he opened Seven Sins, an elite BDSM club, I researched. His kink was no secret to me and Cayleigh, our sister, but I never found it appealing— until I read about it. Until I finally experienced what it was like having a woman kneel before me, willing to do anything I wanted.

I'm so vastly different from my brother. So far you'd wonder if we're even related. I am an unapologetic asshole. I enjoy the cries and screams of the girls who take my dick. They all hope I'll put a ring on their finger. But that will never happen. So, the ones who are lucky enough to experience me are chosen for a particular reason — they need to not have any limits when it comes to what I want.

Soon I'll have a new toy to play with.

Madison Parker.

A young, twenty-one-year-old brunette with eyes of cinnamon. When she came into Seven Sins six months ago, I'd just arrived with my sister. That's when I learned who she was when my brother warned me off.

That was the night I vowed that Madison, with her big, brown eyes that shimmered with restrained hunger, would be my target. A good hunter takes his time, moves in slow, and when they least expect it, attacks with vengeance.

I'm almost at Sins when I smile, knowing there'll be a woman ready for me as soon as I walk through the door. Once I park and exit the vehicle Carrick loaned me if I wanted to make use of it, I grab the one thing I'll need for my scene. The need-to-use instrument, namely the blade in the sleek, leather holster on my belt, is ready to slide over lace or silk, unwrapping the beautiful gift beneath.

It's dangerous.

Knife-play is something not every Dominant or Master will do. But I've found solace in it. My mind shuts out the everyday stresses, and I focus solely on the curved, supple body before me. At thirty-seven, I've practiced it for almost ten years. My hand is steady. I trust myself, and I ensure the woman trusts me.

Celine has been coming here every few weeks, and she's used to this scene with me. It took her time before she trusted me, and she's the only one I do it with. For now. I picture Madison when she's laid out before me. I see her pretty eyes and long, chestnut waves. But Celine, who's sitting at the bar when I enter the club, took a month before she ever allowed my knife near her.

"Callan," she purrs. Her hair is the same color as Madison's, and her eyes the same reddish-brown hue. "I thought you wouldn't make it."

"I told you I'd be here, darling." I plant a chaste kiss on her cheek.

Tonight, I need this. I want my mind to go there, to dip into the darkness of the kink with her. To see her back arch, and the slope of her breasts rise and fall. Those rosy nipples harden at my cool touch. I'll revel in her keening cries which will make me hard enough to fuck her.

And all the while, I'll picture another woman.

The one I've become addicted to seeing, to wanting, to craving.

"Are you ready?" she asks, her lips purse into a full pout.

"I need a drink first. Do you want to stay here or go to my place?"

She shrugs, smiling at me as she sips her pink drink. "Doesn't matter where you take me; we'll still have fun."

Nodding, I order my drink from Dylan and settle on the stool. My muscles are tense. I need a release, and Celine will be just that.

"Want to play a little game?" I question, glancing

at her. There's a look in her eye that tells me she's ready to do anything I ask.

"Sure."

"Meet me in the leather room in ten minutes." I rise, downing the drink and heading to the back of the club. It's busy, so I must slip through the crowd to get to the doorway for the one place I know I can let loose.

I pull off my jacket and unbutton my shirt. The thick leather belt I'm wearing is tugged from the loops as I drop it on the bed. When the whoosh of the door sounds behind me, I don't turn, but the scent of her perfume assaults me.

Spinning on my heel, I don't find the familiar eyes of Celine, but instead, Madison Parker is standing in the doorway dressed in a flowing, knee-length dress.

"What are you doing here?" I ask, shocked at the fact that she's come to the back rooms, somewhere she's never ventured with anyone else before.

"You wanted me in the club—"

"Tomorrow. I can't do this with you now," I inform her.

She steps closer, shutting the door behind her, and

I wonder if she even realizes she's just stepped into the lion's den. "Why?" Her question is slight, almost shy, but there's a fire dancing in her gaze that tells me she's not scared of me at all.

She is beautiful and I do want her, but Oliver warned me to be careful.

His warning echoes in my mind once more, reminding me to be on my guard around her. "Do you like playing with fire?" I question, causing her to slide her gaze up to mine.

"I'm not afraid of getting burned," she says. "Sometimes it's the only way to feel something." Her words, the way she smiles sadly, make me step backward. There's so much more to this woman than meets the eye.

"You should leave."

"Why?" She slowly slips the straps of her dress over her shoulders. It pools to the floor in a heap at her feet. Her legs are encased in black stockings, the thick bands swirl around her upper thighs. The charcoal lingerie, a soft silk camisole she's wearing, is almost see-through, offering me a glimpse of her pink, rosy nipples and that mound that's got dark hair trimmed to perfection. She's all fucking woman, and my dick is ready to play.

It's too soon.

She steps out of the dress and stalks toward me. As soon as our bodies are aligned, she looks up into my eyes then slowly drops to her knees before me.

"Why don't you show me?" Her plump lips move, and the earth fucking tilts on its axis. She's a seductress. A tease.

I reach for her, fisting her long, brown hair in my hand, and yank her head backward. I will never be topped from the bottom. Not by anyone.

"Listen to me very carefully, Madison," I hiss in her face. "When and how I fuck you will be up to me. Not you. If you so much as try to force my hand, I'll make sure that you never get what you so desperately want."

"And what is that?" she whimpers as I feel the strands of her silky hair between my fingers.

"You want me to fuck you so hard, so fucking deep that all the hidden agony you hold inside will disappear."

Her lips part in shock. I can see right through her. I can see her soul crying out for it.

"Remember, sweetheart, I'm in charge. And when

I want you, that's when I'll have you. Now go run back to Daddy and your boyfriend. We'll play tomorrow."

I release my hold on her and saunter into the attached bathroom and shut the door behind me with a smirk on my face. Everything is falling into place. She's at my beck and call, and soon, I'll shatter her.

SIX

MADISON

The door shuts with a resounding click behind him. My body is still trembling when I rise to my feet. My scalp stings from his harsh treatment, but he hasn't scared me. He's only made me want to taunt him more, to see just how far he'll go.

I've spent my life around men like him. The danger that seems to emanate from him is the same menace I see in the eyes of the men my father has working for him. They've seen things that would make most cringe. They've also probably done things that would scare away even the bravest of souls.

The only difference between them and Callan is that he wants me. Even in the anger-filled words he spewed at me, there was an inflection of want in his voice that made my heart thud against my ribs.

I pull the black dress up and over my shoulders, allowing my gaze to drink in the room where he was waiting on the brunette I saw with him at the bar. My choice to come here was my own, to see if he'd be here. When I walked in and ordered my drink, I found a table in the corner where I could watch everyone who walked in. I was about to leave when he sauntered into the club.

As I make my way by the bar toward the exit, I notice the woman he sat with earlier is still there, reaching for her pink drink. I'm tempted to talk to her, to ask about him, but I don't. Instead, I focus on leaving the club and going back home.

"He wants you." Her voice comes from behind me as I pass by, causing me to whip my head toward her.

"What?"

"Callan." She says his name as if she's far too familiar with him, which has jealousy trickling through me. "He has this thing for you. He let it slip one night while he was fucking me." Her words slice through me, and I wonder just how much she's learned about me.

"He let it slip?"

"Your name. He said your name, and I knew exactly who you were. He's been in here for six long months, and you're the only woman he looks at."

I've never been one of those girls whom others were jealous of. I was also never one of the popular girls, so for this woman to look at me with envy in her gaze, I can't help but feel like I have the upper hand.

It's no secret I want Callan. I want to knock him down to earth. I want him to feel. He's cold, closed off from everything around him, and I have a feeling the only love he's ever offered is to his family.

"Thank you." I smile at her, noting the way she regards me. Warily. As if I'm a threat to her. Granted, I could be. She would be easy to take down. Even though she looks far older than I am, I know I'm stronger physically. But deep down, I'm unsure if I can handle an emotional fight.

I turn and leave her at the bar, mulling the words she uttered in my mind. There's a chilly breeze when I step out of the club. The night is only lit by the business sign and the full moon in the sky.

"Madison Parker." A voice, low and gravelly,

comes from behind me causing me to spin on my heel.

"Who are you?" I question, trying to swallow past the lump in my throat.

He doesn't answer. Instead, he gestures to me to head to my car, which is parked in the far corner of the lot, and he follows me there. I should've parked closer to the door where the security guards could see me, but I didn't want Callan to see me if I'd have arrived the same time he did. When I pull open the driver's door, the man who I've only seen once before places his large meaty hand on the window.

"Don't underestimate my boss's reach, girl," he hisses. "Daddy is not safe on his perch." His threat is clear.

"What do you want?"

"You know exactly what the man who pays my wages wants, Ms. Parker. Boss man is adamant to get exactly what your daddy has. A position on the senate. We need you to tell us about where your father is going, who he's meeting with, and we will make sure you don't come to any harm. If you don't help us, well . . ." His smirk is evil, almost demented. "I'll have to take it violently. And make no mistake, I'd enjoy it. There's a folder in your father's office that my boss needs. It contains information about Mr. Brockovich. It needs to be in my hands when I see you again. You have forty-eight hours."

He spins on his heel, and I watch him disappear into the darkness. When I reach for the car door, I notice my hand shaking violently. I should call my dad and tell him about this, but if I do, he could get hurt.

Blackmail is not what I'd envisioned my father to be involved in. If I can find out who this boss man is, perhaps I can talk to him, make him see reason. But even as I think it, I know it's a lie. Men like that don't believe in reason. I can't tell anyone. He'll hurt me and my dad. As much as he isn't the perfect parent, I still love him. Doesn't every daughter love their dad no matter what?

I slip into the driver's seat and start the engine. I'm still shaking, my body trembling with fear of what the man wants. After the experience inside the club, and the one only moments ago, I feel drained. Exhausted with emotion racing through me at a million miles a second.

Sighing, I turn on the radio, hoping the music

will take my mind off the evening's events. I make my way home slowly as shadows dance along the road. The large gates of our property slide open with a creak of metal, beckoning me into the safety of the mansion. Two security men sit on either side of the fence, offering me a nod in greeting as I inch my way up the long driveway.

I don't know how I'm going to get into my father's study. He's always kept it locked. Off limits. With the time limit, I know I have to try something to get in there. He leaves in a few days on his trip, so I'll need to get in there while he's in the house, and that in itself is not easy.

I exit the car and make my way to the door, opening it gently then stepping over the threshold. Silence greets me, but I know he's somewhere. I toe off my shoes in the foyer and pad silently toward his office, which sits at the back of the house. Hidden in the murky depths of the large mansion.

As soon as I reach the door, I notice it's ajar, but there's a light on inside, which means he's working.

"Yes." His deep voice barrels through me, startling me. "He'll never fucking get it," my father snarls angrily. "That asshole will die before he even thinks about getting his hands on the information. I'll make sure of it. I'm interviewing a prospective bodyguard for her tomorrow. Someone I know will keep her safe."

He's silent for a long while, and I know I shouldn't eavesdrop, but I can't help it.

"Yes, he's dangerous, but with the right amount of money, he will do anything to keep my daughter safe. And if he doesn't, he'll join the last asshole in a grave."

Racing from the door, I speed up the stairs and into my room. My lungs are pulling in air painfully. I knew my father could be cold and heartless, but this is new. Killing people? It's as if I don't know the man who raised me.

My mind is awash with vivid images of my father having people killed as I slip under the covers of my bed moments later. My phone vibrates on the pillow beside me, lighting up the bedroom in a golden glow.

When I unlock the device, I find a message from Callan.

Tomorrow you will scream. I hope you're ready for it.

I don't respond. His words only elicit a flurry of want in my stomach. I close my eyes and smile as I focus on him rather than my father being a killer.

SEVEN

CALLAN

The early morning sky is light gray, the sun hidden from sight as I race down the pier. My legs carrying me closer to home. I love running, always have. My mind is clear, and my body is ready for her.

The tension from last night held my muscles tight in its grip, and when I woke this morning, I knew I'd not be able to be near her without fucking her until she's broken beneath me. Cool air swirls around me as I head into the building.

The elevator is waiting when I reach it and step inside. Pressing the button for the fourth floor, I watch the numbers light up. When the doors open, I make my way to my one-bedroom apartment.

Moments later, I'm in the shower with my mind

on her again. Madison has been running through my thoughts since I first saw her, and I know it won't change, even after I've gotten a taste.

I make quick work of getting dressed, and I'm out the door in no time. Smiling as I slide a leg over my bike, I get the engine purring and humming beneath me. It's not far to my destination, and I can't wait to lay my eyes on her again.

I don't have much to do today, but I had to tell her that because if I spent the day around her, there'd be nothing left by the time the sun set this evening. When I finally park the bike, I swing my leg over it, tug off my helmet, and head toward the store.

I pull out my phone and hit dial on her number. After a few rings, her sweet, melodic voice comes through the line, and my cock awakens, hard and ready. "Hello?" She sounds tentative.

"Blossom," I say quietly as if I'm whispering in her ear. I stand there waiting for her to say something, but all I hear is her soft breaths, which stir the need in my gut. The craving to have her near me, bent over, splayed wide, or just bowing to my every order.

My plan is easy.

Lure her with safety, when in fact, she'll never be safe with me.

I want all of her. To take everything she has to give and walk away.

"Are you with your friends?"

"Yes," she whispers, and I hear the giggling in the background. The thing about Madison is she's not like them. I've watched her. Observed who she really is, and it's not those prissy, rich girls who want to wear the latest name brands. No, she's reserved. Quiet and shy. Just the way I like my girls.

"I want to make you all wet for me right now. Would you like that?"

"I-I can't—"

"Madison, I don't like when you deny me what you and I both know you want. You'll listen and obey my orders soon enough because that's what you crave. Isn't it?"

She's silent for so long I wonder if she will actually back out, but then I hear her sigh of resignation. My gruff commands are what she enjoys. "Yes, it is."

"I know. When I finally get to see you later, I look forward to inhaling your sweet arousal like a perfume," I tell her as I make my way toward the coffee shop I saw on Google Maps last night. She doesn't see me pass by the window where she's shopping with her friend, Amber, but she's not meant to.

For years I've perfected my skills at blending in. Most call me a stalker, but I like to think of myself as thorough. I make sure I know my target better than they know themselves.

"And what did you have in mind?" she whispers over the line. I hear a door shutting from her side, and I realize she's alone in a dressing room.

"That's for me to know and you not to find out until it's happening. I like to play games, Blossom. Very naughty games." Once again, she sighs. It's a sound that seems to be linked directly to my cock. Hardening it further behind the zipper of my jeans.

"And what if I don't like your games?"

"You will. That's why you wanted a ride on my bike that night. Good girls want to do bad things with dangerous men. You're a good girl and I'm a very dangerous man," I tell her easily. It's true.

I have my plan for the pretty little Madison Parker.

"I look forward to our meeting, Blossom," I tell her. I hang up, knowing I'll soon be in the Parker house. When Oliver told me about the interview, I knew it was the perfect opportunity. And soon I'll be with her all day, every day.

I know this will be a walk in the park. Working security for someone like him will be easier than the shit I did back home for my father. I pay for the coffee and slowly make my way through the crowd. They're leaving the store with bags of clothes, and I watch her from the shadows. She doesn't even look my way as she follows the blonde she calls a friend down the road.

I savor the coffee while my gaze drinks her in.

She's exquisite in every way. Too perfect for me. But I've learned a long time ago that perfection is merely a smokescreen. There's always imperfections beneath a shiny surface.

Once I'm back where I parked, I'm on my Ducati starting the engine with a loud roar. The streets are busy, but being without a car, it's easy for me to zip through the traffic. There's nothing I love more than feeling the power between my legs. Actually, scratch that. There is one more thing I'd prefer between my legs, and her name is Madison Parker.

Last night, she was a temptation. Something I couldn't touch, because I knew today I'd be meeting with her daddy dearest, and soon, I'll know exactly who her pussy-ass boyfriend is. Once I've weaseled my way into her house, into her life, she'll soon be rid of him, and I'll be the one making her moan. But most of all, I'll be the one keeping her safe, until I crack the pedestal and watch her father fall from grace.

When I pull up to the three-story mansion, I find four security guards dressed in black suits with white shirts parked off doing fuck-all. They all look like they're on vacation instead of protecting my girl's home.

"Callan O'Leary here to see Mr. Parker," I inform one of the suits who crooks his finger for me to step closer. He frisks my shoulders, back, and around my waist. He rises to full height, still measuring in a few inches shorter than me.

"You're clear," he grumbles in the mic sitting on

the side of his head. He steps aside, allowing me to walk my bike down the drive.

The house is enormous. Granted, we did have a manor house in England, and this could easily pass for the same. The gardens are perfectly manicured, with blossoms of roses, jasmine, azalea bushes, patchouli, and even weeping cherry line the drive. Everything is too beautiful on the outside, which makes me smile because I know what sordid little lies are hidden on the inside.

There's no one else around besides the security I met at the gate a few hundred feet down. A creak of wood sounds behind me, causing me to turn around. There in the doorway is Mr. Magnus Parker. The US Senator for five years running.

"Mr. O'Leary," he smirks, his expensive suit tailored to fit his short, pudgy frame.

"That would be me," I tell him, my accent thick, gravelly.

He steps closer, gripping my hand firmly as he shakes it. His eyes, the color of coal, watch me with a wariness I always get when I'm around strangers. I may be the villain in most respects, but I never fucking hide it.

"Come," he says, leading me into the house where I'm sure he not only lives but works too, and possibly even hides whatever vile secrets politicians hide. The interior is everything I pictured — pristine, cream walls with vintage artwork hanging down the hallways we silently veer along to reach his office.

Each piece of furniture looks like it belongs in an old Scottish castle rather than in the modern home of a US Senator. He doesn't speak, merely ambles along ahead of me as if he's the goddamn president. Only standing at five feet nine, he's shorter than me, but there's a commanding aura about the man.

I follow him into what I'm guessing is his office.

"Please, take a seat," he tells me as he makes his way around the ornate cherry wood desk. It's large, taking over most of the space. The room itself reminds me of my father's office, dark and dreary. Most of the older men in politics and organized crime think it comes across as foreboding. Me, I think they're all just fucking around trying to be scary when they're actually more shit-scared of the younger generation taking over.

"I understand you're looking for a man who can act as security as well as chauffeur?" I question, watching him settle into his expensive seat. The onyx leather creaks as his heavy frame fills the space.

He regards me through narrowed cocoa eyes. Lifting his hands, he steeples them before him, heightening his chin somewhat. Even with the added height, the flabby, wrinkled skin still hangs from his face.

"I want someone reliable who can watch her. She's running rogue with these girls she's been friends with, and it's tarnishing my reputation. Oliver told me you're the best in the business, and I trust him." His voice is filled with frustration, almost as if Madison was a teenager heading out to clubs and getting pregnant. No, she's not that at all. She's so far removed from that life, and I don't think her father even knows what a good girl he has. And he knows exactly who Amber is. This feined concern is bullshit.

Judgment is never easy to come to terms with. Especially when it comes from family. From those you love the most. It sucks you dry, moment by soul destroying moment.

Tipping my head to the side, I watch him for a minute before leaning forward. My elbows hit my knees as I steady myself. I'm tempted to knock the fucker out. He knows nothing about his daughter, but there he sits, acting as if he's the best father in the world when I know his concerns about Amber are bullshit. He's not worried about her influence on his daughter, and I know why.

"And what makes you think she's in need of someone like that?"

"There's talk of her attending a club downtown that's got me concerned. I trust that with your background, you can both keep an eye on her as well as find out what it is she's up to when she goes there. Her friends are a bad influence on her."

He stares at me hard then, and I know there's something he's not telling me. The tension in his shoulders and the curve of his pursed lips hold secrets he's not divulging to me. And that's not how this works.

Nodding, I confirm, "I can do that. However, I need honesty. I'm not talking about telling me the shit you think is going on. I don't work well under a ruse." I rise, stalking over to the windows to the right of his desk. They overlook the vast gardens of his property. From here, the city sits quietly in the distance, alive with promise.

"Look, Madison is my baby girl. She's young, impressionable and . . ." His voice trails off into nothing, causing me to turn to him. "Her friends are rather risqué. I'm concerned about her safety, and I know you'd be the man to keep her out of harm's way."

"I can certainly do that, but I'm not a babysitter. If she wants to go shopping with friends, I'm not one to stop her." I chuckle, earning me a glare, but I don't give a shit.

"Also, I'd like her to find time for Hudson. He's a good boy. One of my best. She's been rather standoffish toward him, and I'm concerned." He's actually telling me to play fucking matchmaker. That's definitely way outside my paygrade.

"Listen to me, Mr. Parker," I order, making my way to the desk. Placing both palms flat on the cool wooden surface, I lean in, meeting his brown eyes. "Your daughter will be under my care. I'll watch her, keep her safe, and ensure nothing bad happens to her. I'll drive her wherever she needs to go, but make no mistake, I'm not here to play matchmaker." *But I will fuck her tight body until she's broken*, I add in my mind.

"That's fine, but I want to remind you she's precious to me. But I like your confidence, Mr. O'Leary," he smirks, sitting back like a king on his throne. "You start tomorrow. I'll introduce you to Madi in the morning. Be here at nine, sharp. I have meetings all day, and you'll have to drive her around, be her shadow." He reaches out a hand to me, which I grab. We shake on the agreement. Once I release his hand, I step back, allowing him to rise. "This is your contract," he says, tossing a thick folder on the desk before me. "Read it, sign it, bring it along tomorrow, and we'll get you set up with one of the SUVs."

"You won't be sorry," I inform him.

"I know. I've looked into your background after being referred by Oliver Michaelson. I know you're good at what you do, and I trust you'll look after my daughter."

"Always." I offer him a nod before grabbing my contract and heading out the door. I'm escorted by two suits toward the exit. Once outside, I can't help smirking. I've landed the job, which was all part of the plan.

I'll be right beside little Madi all day, every day.

Two hours later, when I walk into Sins, I find Mason and Rick sitting at one of the booths with mugs of coffee and paperwork strewn all over the table. It looks like they're deep in conversation when I stroll over to them.

I read through the contract twice to make sure that every T was crossed and every I was dotted. There's something about accomplishing something that you've been planning for months. Since I first saw Madison here six months ago, I knew I had to have her. A normal man would just go up to her and ask her on a date, but I'm not a normal man.

I'm far from it.

I prefer the chase, the taunting and teasing.

And when I finally catch my prey, I devour them.

Pulling up a chair, I spin it and straddle the seat,

leaning my elbows on the back. "What's happening in here?" I question, meeting my brother's gaze.

"We're discussing the possibility of a new recruit."

"Oh?" I lean forward, grabbing my brother's tumbler, which is already swirling with amber liquid. "And what exactly does this job entail?"

"Security. You interested, brother?" Rick questions, glancing at me curiously.

"Me? I actually just signed a contract for a new job. I'll be security detail."

"Oh yeah? Who's it with?" Mason questions, opening one of the manila folders on the table.

"Senator Parker actually," I tell them.

My brother's gaze snaps to me with confusion dancing in his gold eyes. "What?"

"Yeah, he needs a new driver-slash-bodyguard for his precious little girl." I chuckle.

Carrick groans. Sitting back, he regards me, narrowing his eyes into taunting slits. "You planned it. Didn't you?"

I don't respond. Instead, I shrug and glance at Mason. "So, what's that?" I ask, gesturing to the folder with my chin.

He hands it to me and I flip through the basic requirements. The standard details seem easy enough, but I notice the times and finer details will need to be changed. "Your brother said you're good with security detail. You've done this before, and I trust that since you are family, you'll be happy to work here. We just need you in the evenings. I'm sure your new boss won't have you working twenty-four seven."

"I'm sure that will be fine. When do you leave?" I question my brother.

"Next week. Flights are booked."

I take in my brother's expression, and I see the happiness on his face. I haven't seen him this happy in years, but Peyton has been good for him. "I'll make sure I'm around when I'm needed," I tell him.

"Great. You can start work on Wednesday." My brother's best friend informs me, holding out his hand. My eyes drift between him and Rick.

"Take it. That means you'll be able to keep an eye on Leigh as well as your little dolly," Carrick taunts me. I used to call my teenage girlfriend Dolly because she was as pretty as one. "I've decided to take Peyton to Europe. We'll probably head over to see Dad as well."

"You're going to London?" My question comes out filled with shock. I never pictured my brother ever returning to the place he walked out of. It's been years, and he never looked back. But knowing he's taking Peyton there, that's more shocking than anything. Not because she doesn't deserve to see where we grew up, but when Dad sees her, he'll lose his shit.

She looks just like Rick's ex-fiancée who was killed at my sister's wedding over nine years ago now.

"You want me to babysit Cayleigh? You do realize she's going to give me the slip as soon as she can." My little sister is a little firecracker. She's been like that since she was a teenager. There's never been a time that I knew my sister not to be in trouble with our parents.

Sadly, losing mom was difficult for her, and that's when she really went off the rails. Carrick and I had to step in and be the older brothers who put our foot down. Since then, she's slowly calmed down. Her partying has dwindled into nothing, and I wonder if being here will turn her into the party girl from her younger years.

"I just need you to watch over her. Also, we need someone we can trust in the club. Since Mason will be on his own, I'd much prefer you being here with him. This is yours as much as it is mine, brother," Rick tells me.

"Fine, I'll be here for her and for the club. Thank you for thinking of me. Us working together again will be a challenge." I chuckle, slapping Rick on the shoulder.

His smirk is enough to tell me he's happy with the choice. It's been a long time since the O'Leary brothers were together.

"Tell me, why Anderson?" I question. My brother changed his last name when he moved here. I know deep down he hated where he came from, the life he was forced to live, and when he lost Aurora, it shattered everything he believed in.

He shrugs. "It was easy. I needed something that wouldn't tie me to home."

"You mean to the mob," I tease, winking as I rise. Pushing the chair to the side, I pull out my smokes and lighter. "I'm heading out. I'll be by tomorrow to sign the contract."

"Great. Mason will get it ready for you, and you'll

officially be staff of Seven Sins," Carrick tells me with a smile. "And remember, no fighting. Just keep the peace while I'm gone."

"Peace? With Leigh? You know she's worse than a kid on a candy high," I retort, earning myself a chuckle. It's true though, and Carrick knows it. I pull out my phone, tapping out a message to my new toy, telling her I can't wait to see her. However, I don't tell her I'll be her new bodyguard. That's a surprise I want to spring on her while I'm staring into those honey-colored eyes.

"Just watch out for her."

"I'll catch you later, I have to make plans for tonight. I have a flower to pick, and I can't wait to inhale those sweet petals," I tell them, turning to leave.

Carrick calls out to me before I make my way toward the exit. "Stay away from Madison Parker." I don't respond. Instead, I head out into the warm afternoon sunshine. My brother knows me too well. Anytime he's told me not to do something, I've made sure to do exactly that. This time it will be no different.

EIGHT

MADISON

It's almost time. I don't see him, but he may be in the back somewhere. When he told me to meet him in Sins, I knew tonight he'd finally take me. Give me what I want and need.

To say I'm nervous is an understatement. With each person who walks in, my heart leaps into my throat. Tonight, I'll ask Callan to take me to the back room, any of them, and make good on his promises. All those filthy words he spewed, I want them. I ache for them.

Two men stalk into the club with a beautiful blonde girl between them. She looks like she's my age, perhaps a year or two younger, which would put her just at legal age. My twenty-one years makes me prime meat in this place.

I note that most of the Dominants who are in here have a younger girl on their arm. Or sitting on their laps. The lights in the club dim, and a beautiful woman steps up onto the stage. She's exquisite with her long, dark hair and curvaceous body wrapped in a deep blue dress.

I watch her as she introduces Mason and Savannah. One of the owners of Seven Sins along with his beautiful submissive Savvie perform rope scenes on stage which have always intrigued me, and I wonder what it would feel like to be suspended like that. But even though my gaze is locked on them, all I can think about is seeing him.

I've never been this nervous before because it's always been Hudson. The rather mechanical man who my father is convinced is perfect for me. When he first kissed me, I felt the chill in the way his lips touched mine, and I knew there'd never be passion between us.

It's been far too long since I've felt a rush of danger. Adrenaline coursing through my veins. And sadly, it's been a long time since I've ever wanted to be kissed by someone, or even touched.

Not those gentle caresses that some girl's dream

about. I'm talking about a rough, manhandled grip. As if he's trying to tell you he owns you with a simple touch. I've been thinking about Callan all night, all day. Even with Amber rambling on about the dresses she was trying on, it was him on my mind.

I know this isn't a date. I doubt he's ever been on one.

He's not the type.

I rise slowly, lifting my empty glass, and head to the bar. I can't sit still anymore. Every moment that passes makes me more anxious. It's as if I'm undercover and I'm waiting on my mark to arrive.

My eyes flit over the crowd once more after I've ordered my drink, seeking him out, but I feel his gaze on me before I find him. He's behind me in an instant. He leans in, allowing his lips to feather across my cheek.

"Hello, Blossom," he murmurs in a low gravelly tone that wraps itself around me.

"Callan," I breathe his name. He plants a kiss on my cheek then spins me around. Coming face to face with him is like being electrocuted. He's rough everywhere. Dark stubble dusts his jaw. Those eyes, deep and feral, root me to the spot. Thick, black lashes frame his midnight-blue eyes, and his lips purse into a grin that both scares me and turns me on.

"I didn't think you'd make it," he states. There's a satisfied smirk on his face, and I wonder if he's enjoying this. Our banter, teasing, whatever you want to call it.

"Why wouldn't I?"

He shakes his head. "Thought you'd be too scared of me."

"I'm not some innocent little girl, Callan. I told you, I'm not scared of anything." My retort earns me a sexy chuckle. "What?" I question his curious gaze.

"Nothing," he says, turning to the barman, offering him a grin. "D, get me a Jameson. Make it a double." The young man behind the bar nods and busies himself getting the drink, but I note the glimpses he shoots our way.

I want to say something to Callan, anything, but my tongue feels heavy. My stomach has a flurry of butterflies awakening from a long slumber, and my heart is no longer beating a regular rhythm.

Once we have our drinks, Callan places his hand at

the base of my spine and ushers me down a long hallway.

"Are we going to—"

"Tell me, Madison," he interrupts me without so much as a blink. He shoves a black door open, and we find ourselves in a decadent room with a large bed decked in sheets the color of Merlot. Black leather and silver metal furnish the space. It should be scary, but it's not, and I find myself intrigued more than fearful. "Why did you come to me outside the club? And don't tell me it's because you wanted a ride."

A blush heats my cheeks, traveling down my neck, but he can't see it because I'm looking at the instruments hanging against the wall. Two leather cuffs are attached to what I know to be a St. Andrews Cross. My eyes drop to my chest, and with the low-cut dress I'm wearing, it does nothing to hide the flush on my skin.

I turn to face him. He's drenched in darkness and shadows. But that's who he is. That's where his past lies. I don't know much about it, but from the folder of info my father's PI found, I know Callan O'Leary must have a treacherous past.

"I . . ." There's no other way to say this, so I swallow

my anxiety and glance up at his dark eyes. "I wanted to see if you're as dangerous as you looked. I noticed you a couple of months ago when I was with Amber, and she said you're probably a serial killer."

A sound vibrates through his chest at my admission. A low, gravelly chuckle. "And do you make it your life's purpose to go around teasing serial killers?"

"No, of course not. I just . . . I felt like . . . I don't know, like I wanted to know you. Is that so difficult to understand?" He stalks toward me, closing the distance in an instant. His frame is large, strong, and it cocoons my smaller one.

"I got a job today," he tells me, not answering my question.

"O-kay," I drag out the word, confused at why he's telling me this. He places a hand on my hip, and the other finds my chin, tilting it up so I'm looking directly at him. Maybe he's going to tell me he really is a serial killer, and I'm on his hit list.

"You may know my boss," he utters, but doesn't offer more. My brows kick together in confusion before he tells me a name that causes my mouth to fall open.

"Mr. Parker."

"What? My father?" I step back, but his hand juts out, gripping my wrist. He tugs me closer, his body molding to mine, or is it mine that's clearly so needy for him I'm pressing my curves against him? I place my hand on his chest, pushing him backward, needing space. As much as I want him near me, against me, inside me, I also have to think.

"Don't go running off now," he warns, but my gaze is pinned on him, questioning him with just one look. "Yes, I'm working for your father, but in essence, I'm at your service." His smile lights up his rather dark demeanor. The steely expression he normally has plastered on his face changes. There are wrinkles in the corners of his eyes. His lips, full, pink, curl into a boyish grin. Even though he looks far too old for me, I can't help noticing how handsome he is.

"What do you mean?"

"I'll be your new security detail, chauffeur," he says smugly. His face a picture of devilish intent and naughty satisfaction.

"Callan, I don't need—"

He cuts me off by tugging me against his solid frame. My hands landing on his shoulders, feeling the muscle tighten and bulge. The response of my body to him, to his touch is scorching. And this time I can't push away because I want this.

He leans in so close I can smell the alcohol on his warm breath.

"You do need," he murmurs. "You do want. And trust me when I say this, I'm about to deliver."

Gently, he brushes his lips along mine. It's not a kiss — it's torture. My body hums, my blood heats, and my panties near enough disintegrate. His hands are rough, calloused, but his mouth is inviting, tempting. Too sinful to even think about because he shouldn't be doing this.

If my father saw me now, saw us now, he'd have Callan killed or worse. They think I don't know about the shady shit my father does, and I wonder if my new bodyguard has any inkling. As quickly as his mouth finds mine, it disappears. He moves away, releasing my hips.

"Tonight, we play. Are you ready?" he questions me.

"I've been ready for a while." My response earns me

a chuckle.

He gestures to the chair. "Sit." It's an order, and so the game begins. I move to the ornate wingback chair, which reminds me of the stormy clouds on a winter's day. Once I'm perched on the plush cushion, he turns to grab his drink. "Now, I want you to lift your skirt." There's a coldness, almost brashness to his command, but I obey.

With trembling fingers, I lift the hem of my dress, knowing he'll soon see what I've hidden for so long from everyone but Hudson. His gaze burns my skin as it follows the track of the material. The growl that vibrates through his chest tells me he's noticed them, and I don't know what he's going to do now.

"Sit back and open your legs," he bites out but doesn't make mention of the scars he's seen.

He's so calm. But the muscles of his arms bulge as they tense under the crisp white material of his shirt. There's tension rolling through his muscles as his hands fist, causing the veins to pop out, and I wonder what he looks like naked.

I spread my legs, my stomach tumbling as he

watches me eagerly. There's a hunger in his gaze. A grunt rumbles in his chest when he sees my lace panties. The bright orange color matches my bra, the skimpy material barely covering my pussy. They're tight, revealing, and drenched.

Callan is all man. Strong, foreboding, but also handsome. He slowly unbuttons his shirt. Moving so torturously slow I want to beg him to hurry. I want to see him. Naked, but also needy for me as I am for him.

His strong hands tug the material from the waistband of his jeans. They hug his muscled thighs; the dark fabric looks like it's been painted on. When his shirt finally hits the floor, I'm met with the beautifully chiseled man who has me squirming as I trail my gaze over him. Corded veins are prominent on his hands and up his arms, making my mouth water.

"Do you like the view, sweetheart?" he smirks confidently. There's so much about this man that makes me want to slap him for being so arrogant, but it's that quality that makes me want him so much more.

"You're far too confident, Mr. O'Leary," I tell him, allowing my fingers to tease my sex.

His gaze drops between my legs, not mentioning my imperfections. "If you touch your pretty pussy again, I'll make sure you beg me to stop tonight," he warns. There's an underlying threat, one that sets my body alight. "But you like that, don't you?"

He stalks closer, his body only inches from mine when he rips my hand from between my legs. I'm about to pull my skirt down, but his large calloused fingers grip me painfully.

"Is that what you hide from everyone?" he grits out through clenched teeth. "Answer me, Madison, or I swear to god I'll fucking punish you so badly you'll need an ambulance to leave here tonight."

My mouth falls open, but I can't find my confidence to respond. Tears sting my eyes when he glares, the heat of his eyes trickle over me like flames licking at a piece of paper, and I'm afraid I'm about to go up in smoke.

"It's . . . I need it, Callan." My whisper is barely audible, and I'm sure he hasn't heard, but a moment later, he shakes his head.

"That's bullshit, Madison." The low, menacing growl that leaves his lips is enough to have my heart leaping into my throat, threatening to choke me.

"It's none of your business," I hiss, pushing him away. I don't need this. All my life I've been judged. First for my body, then from my so-called boyfriend for my coping mechanism.

Callan rips me out of the chair seconds later and drags me, literally fucking drags me to the St. Andrews Cross. He binds me to the leather apparatus, and even though I'm cursing him, he ignores me.

My wrists are taut against the contraption, my ankles are spread wide, and I'm standing on my tip toes to keep my hands from losing feeling.

"What the fuck are you doing?" I bite out, anger and desire all swirling together in a maelstrom of an impending disaster. I feel like there's a storm coming, and I'm not prepared. The name of the hurricane is Callan O'Leary. He stalks off, leaving me there for long moments. When he finally returns, he seems far too calm. In his hand, he's gripping a leather whip that only makes my anxiety peak.

"What is your safe word?"

I meet his intense stare and spit the word at him.

"Wrath."

The corner of his mouth quirks into a sinful grin. One so fucking handsome, so downright gorgeous all I want is to see him between my thighs.

"Oh, Blossom, when I'm done with you, you'll indeed be wanting vengeance." His promise, a vow to cause me pain, doesn't scare me. He doesn't fucking scare me.

"Do your worst," I taunt.

He lifts his hand, and the leather licks my skin, again and again. I count in my head, but when I reach ten, I lose it. I can't think straight.

"Callan!"

He stalls for a moment, drops the whip, and I think my punishment is over, but it's not. It's far from it. His hands grip my face, holding me in place. Even though I can't move my limbs or my body, his hold on my face is what leaves me paralyzed.

"If you ever, and I fucking mean ever hurt yourself," he hisses, the deep baritone of his voice vibrating through me, "I'll whip you so hard that you bleed. I'll watch the pretty crimson drip from your flesh."

"Please," I whimper. I'm unsure of what I'm asking of him, what I want, but there's something I need from him. An ache low in my belly starts, and I can feel the arousal dripping from me.

He releases me, reaches to his side, and then he's back in front of me. So close I can smell the spicy cinnamon scent of his cologne.

"Now," he starts. "I'm going to do something I've never done with a girl in our first scene." He pulls out a blade, shiny and luminous in the dim light. "Is this what you used to fuck-up your perfect body?"

"Fuck you, Callan," I bite out, my anger fueling my speech, making me spew out words of rage rather than desire.

"Tell me," he insists. "I want to hear it from your lips." His taunting causes me to cry out. I should call out my safe word. I should make him stop, but he's seen right through me. He's looked into the very depth of my soul, and I have no way of getting him out.

"I needed to feel," I sob. When I finally blink, tears stream down my face. But he doesn't relent. He lifts the blade, placing it on the curve of my breasts. Gently, he trails it over the flesh, causing me to shudder.

I watch it move over my body, the hypnotic feeling of the steel against me makes me want more, I need him to press harder, to see the sweet crimson release of letting go of pain, but he doesn't. Instead, the gentle scrapes make their way to my stomach. When he reaches between my legs, I pull in a harsh breath.

The panties I was wearing fall to the floor, and I'm now bared to him. Open and wanton. He doesn't say anything. Instead, he presses a kiss to my mound, then harshly swats my wet pussy with his large hand, causing me to cry out loudly.

He takes his knife, the blade against my smooth flesh, just above my clit. "I'm here, Madison, because for some inexplicable reason you've caught my eye," he confesses, not looking at me. But rather, his rapt attention is on the sleek blade. His fingers twist it round and round, allowing it to scratch against me slightly, which only makes me wetter.

"And that's a bad thing?" I smile, but when he lifts his deep blue eyes to meet mine, I see the war raging within those dark pools.

"It's a very bad thing, Blossom."

"Why?" I challenge, leaning forward, but I can only move an inch before my wrists protest.

Callan's eyes darken further when his fingers push into my core. It's not far enough for me to feel filled, but it's enough to make me whimper. By the time he shakes his head, I meet his gaze and find both orbs black as night before he averts them. "Because you're not mine to take," he finally tells me.

I consider his words for a moment. Granted, I'm not the most experienced girl out there, but I know what he means. He wants to have me, to fuck me, to devour me, just like I want him to. The only thing that stops us is my father. Hudson is not part of the reasoning that Callan has. He's not my boyfriend. He's nothing to me.

"And now I work for you, I should keep things professional." His words are pained. He wants me as much as I do him.

"I'm not going to make it easy on you to resist me," I warn, earning me a sinful smirk.

He nods, the weapon in his hand now pressing against my core. The handle pushes against my bare lips as he taunts my body with it.

"Do you wish this was my dick?" He chuckles as he pushes an inch inside me.

"You shouldn't taunt me," I tell him, thankful he's not asking about the scars on my legs and stomach. I don't need affection. I want it rough. I need to feel something other than the guilt and agony that sits in my mind constantly.

"I like to taunt little girls," he says. "And when you look at me with those big brown eyes, it makes me want to do filthy things to you. It makes me want to feel your slick walls tighten around my cock."

"Then do it," I bite out. My body needy and wanting to be filled by him.

He clutches my throat, squeezing the breath from my lungs, and I hear the knife clatter to the cabinet inches from us. The hiss of a zipper sound, and seconds later, I feel the slickness of his cock against me.

"I thought you said you can't have me?" I tease, watching him, waiting for that inkling that tells me he was lying. A small flicker in his eyes confirms I'm right. He wants the job, but he wants something more. Me.

"Oh, Blossom, I can't have you since I signed your Daddy's contract, but that doesn't make me care. I'm not proclaiming love, I'm not even giving you a fucking ring." He brings a foil packet to his lips and rips it with his teeth. He releases my neck as he sheaths himself.

When his eyes find mine once more, he smirks.

"What I am going to do is make you come so hard your knees will give out, your eyes will roll back, and all you remember is my name." Then he leans in closer, his lips feather along my cheek. "There are times in my life I've taken anything I wanted. I didn't care about those I hurt or even killed, and this time"— he plants a rough kiss on my cheek, his cock nudging me, warning me, and I almost cry out for more — "this time, is no different. You're too perfect to fuck up, but I'll be damned if I don't get a taste of you. All I want to do is violate you every fucking day."

With that illicit promise, he drives into my pussy, and I do scream. I cry out his name over and over again, and his hips piston into me.

His hand once more finds my throat. He chokes me. He makes my pussy squeeze his cock as he thrusts into me. My body is open for him, and all I can think about is his how deep he is, how good the sting of the pain feels inside me.

The cold metal is back, and I lose myself in the way he trails the knife over my nipples, pressing against the sensitive skin that's puckered and hard for him.

"Hold tight, Blossom. Can't be losing your petals," he murmurs against my neck, and I'm so damn close. His cock, thick and hard, violates me in the most delicious of ways, offering me everything I need as it hits the spot inside that has my toes curling and my throat hoarse from the pleas falling from my lips.

I've never experienced just letting go. Callan takes my body and abuses it. His mouth latches onto my shoulder, his teeth grazing the flesh, and I ache for the pain. I moan it out, begging him for more.

My eyes are closed, the darkness sparks with bright lights as he presses the handle of his knife against my puckered entrance and growls when I beg for more. I want him to use me. I need him to violate me. And I crave for him to own me.

I'm filled suddenly. The pain sears me for a moment

and tears sting my eyes as I scream his name like a chanting prayer. Like I'm meditating and he's the only thing to ground me, and he does. He offers me that and so much more.

His cock slams into me. Taking me over an edge I didn't know existed, and my body explodes, trembling and shaking and squirting my release all over him, drenching him in my musky scent.

"Callan," I rasp as I feel his cock throb and pulse inside me, and I know he's found his bliss with me.

"Just enjoy it," he whispers quietly. And my traitorous heart agrees. She likes this. As dangerous as it is, she wants him, this, and everything we're doing tonight.

NINE

CALLAN

I should walk out. Leave her here while she gets dressed and rights herself, but I don't. When I slip from her body, she whimpers at the loss, and something inside me jerks to life. Emotions I've long shoved aside.

I was lost to the world my father created for me for so long, wanting a normal life just seems trivial. Killing someone came easily to me. Carrick wasn't like me. He was softer than I ever was. My heart had been cold since the day I turned sixteen. I never wanted to be like our father. But the day that changed me forever enforced what I would become. When I saw what monsters did, I wanted to be the scariest of them all. The men who worked for our father, Padraig O'Leary, watched as the young boy became cold, closed off to everyone around him, and killed for fun.

Silently, I help Madison from the cuffs, lifting her bridal style in my arms. When I set her on the bed, my gaze lingers on her scars. And I feel the pull to her. That invisible tether between us. My scars are hidden within me, deep inside my soul that's been marred for far too long. Only I know they're there.

Reminders of who I am.

Her eyes flutter as she regards me with a soft smile.

"You're lost in your mind again," Madison utters from the bed. I'm dressed, my shirt unbuttoned, but I pull it over my shoulders. I know I should give her aftercare, hold her and tell her she's perfect, but I can't bring myself to do it. I'm bad at this, at being with a woman, but she doesn't seem deterred.

Nodding, I respond, "I do that sometimes."

"Why?" She sounds genuinely curious. Not baiting me, but just innocently wanting to know more. I settle on the bed, placing a hand on her thigh, gently stroking it. My focus is on her flesh, on all the silver marks that mar her perfect skin.

She's hurt herself. There are so many, which causes

me to wonder if she still does it. If she's still hurting inside.

"This," I start, ignoring her question. "Will never happen again. Do you hear me?" This time, I do look at her. There's a gentle defiance in her gaze. I wait for her to refuse me. To tell me I'm not her father, but she doesn't.

"What makes you think I'll ever listen to you?"

Narrowing my gaze at her sassy query, I lean in closer, pulling her lower lip in between mine, biting down on the flesh so hard, she yelps. "Because I'll hurt you if you cut yourself. I'll fucking whip you and offer you the pain you want. But I never want to find out you're doing this to yourself."

"You know, Callan, you act so tough, but you're not." Her words seep through me. They remind me of a person that doesn't exist. A man who feels affection. I raise my hand, bringing it down on her leg with a loud smack.

I rise, grabbing the knife I dropped earlier, bringing it to her chest. Her tits rise and fall as her breathing hitches.

"What are you doing?"

I press the tip between both mounds of flesh, just a tiny prick to draw out her blood. I pull the knife away and lean in, lapping at the droplet of crimson.

"God," she whimpers making my eyes snap to hers in alarm.

"Did you like that, Blossom?"

A blush turns her cheeks red, the same color I want to see on her ass. I bring the blade back to her body, trailing it down her flat stomach, over the dip of her belly button, causing her to squirm.

"If you move, you'll get hurt," I warn her, and she listens, lying on her back, watching me like I'm her savior. I reach her mound, gently pressing on the smooth caramel skin. She's so fucking exquisite. "Open your legs." My voice is gruff as I order her to spread herself for me. "You're my first, Blossom. The first woman who I've allowed to see my dark side so soon," I confess easily as I trail the sleek silver over her lips, the moisture of her juices coating the tip of the knife, and my cock hardens for her.

"I've never . . . I mean . . . Callan," she whimpers when I press a finger into her hole. The heat of her, the tightness that sucks me in is enough to have my balls drawing up with another load for her.

"Shh." I plant a kiss on her flesh, snaking my tongue over the smooth lips of her cunt, tasting the sweet muskiness of her arousal as I trail the blade over the flesh along with my tongue. It makes her shiver, and even though she should be scared, I know for a fact she's not.

"Please," she mewls when my tongue darts into her, fucking her with my mouth as I cool her skin with the metal. Her legs splay. She's wide open for me, and I glance up from between her thighs to find her hooded gaze on me.

Her delicate hands grip my hair, pulling me closer as she lifts her hips against me, riding my face like I'm her personal fuck-toy, and god how I want to be. I crave to give this woman so much pleasure.

She continues to mewl as she moves against me, needing the pressure, and I allow her to control the movement. I'm her plaything, and she abuses me as a release shocks her. Seconds later she cries out as she coats my tongue in her juices.

When I rise from her, watching and reveling as I see her thighs tremble uncontrollably, I smirk as she lies boneless on the dark sheets.

"My past is something I've embraced for so long, I don't know how to be anything else," I confess in that moment when I know she may never remember it. I don't know why I'm telling her, but for some reason, this sweet, chestnut-haired girl has unraveled me.

She drifts from the high, meeting my gaze with a question. "And you're still that bad man in your heart?"

This time I nod. "I'm a bad man right down to my soul, Blossom." Pushing off the bed, I turn to look down at her. "Get dressed." She doesn't respond as I make my way into the attached bathroom and shut the door behind me.

The way she looks at me under those dark lashes does something to my chest. It's tight with need for her. Shaking my head, I turn on the tap and splash my face with water. I rinse the knife and place it in the holster attached to my belt.

Once I've taken a piss, I head back into the bedroom to find her dressed, sitting on the bed looking like a lost girl with no one to care for her, and I know that's not something I can offer her. Forever isn't in my vocabulary. What I can give her, though, is something that will give her release from the agony in her soul.

"We'll play," I tell her, not going to her, but instead leaning on the door jamb. "I'll keep you safe because I'm getting paid for it, but don't look at me like I'm your savior."

She rises, lifts her chin, and glares at me. She's angry. That's what I want and need from her. To not offer me her heart because I know I'll break it wide open, and I won't feel an ounce of guilt. It's who I am, who I've always been.

Even though she can see what an asshole I am, she still looks at me with those big eyes filled with hope. I wonder if she looks at her daddy the same way. Or if she knows what type of man he is. The things he does using the position his job has put him in. He's no better than I am, only he doesn't get his hands dirty. He hires people like me to do the dirty work for him.

"I'm not in need of a savior, Callan. But is it so bad that I want to know who you are?" she questions innocently.

"Yes," I tell her adamantly. I hope she'll let this go, but something tells me the little spitfire isn't about to let me walk away without delving into my soul and ripping it apart until she sees the darkness lurking beneath the surface.

I want to tear her sweetness apart with my teeth. Take it from her and bask in it. There's never been a point in my life where I craved a woman. Yes, I've fucked plenty, but they didn't mean anything to me. I never said those three words that most men do when they find the one.

I reach for Madison, pulling her closer. Spinning us around, I push her against the wall with a harsh thud. "I don't do love," I tell her. "I'll only force orgasms on you. I'll make you fucking scream. Do you hear me?"

"Loud and clear," she hisses.

"Good girl. Now go home to Daddy, and I'll see you in the morning." I shove away from her, closing myself off again.

"Why do you push people away?"

She doesn't move, so I step away turning my back

to her. Her phone chimes from her purse, and I thank god for the reprieve of the ache in my groin. I want to fuck her again, to be inside her tight heat. My mind is a mess, and her phone chimes once more.

"You better get that," I bite out in frustration.

"Tell me, Callan." She's adamant, ignoring the incessant ringing which grates on my nerves. "I thought we were—"

"Don't get your hopes up, Blossom. This isn't a fucking date. We fucked, it was fun, scene is over now." I stalk toward the door. My hand on the handle, I glance at her once more and nod toward her purse. "Answer your phone."

She sighs as I tug open the door and pull it shut behind me. I make my way up to the apartment Rick offered me and Cayleigh when we arrived. Pushing open the door, I find my sister on the sofa reading. She's always had her nose buried in a book, ever since she was old enough to read.

She glances up at me then wrinkles her nose. "What are you doing here?"

"Needed some fresh air," I tell her, settling on the

armchair, which faces where she's sitting. She doesn't say anything for a moment, then meets my gaze.

"Does this have something to do with the pretty girl?"

I stare at her, wondering how much she knows. I haven't told anyone about Madison, except Carrick, and I know he'd never say anything. God, he'd probably have me locked up for what I did to her in the room moments ago.

"What do you know about it?"

Cayleigh shrugs. "Just asking," she tells me, but there's more she wants to say. I can see it in her eyes. My sister has been through so much, and talking to her about anything other than work is not something I do. For some reason, she listens to my stories about murder rather than wanting to talk about the affection I'd hold for someone.

"I fucked her," I blurt out, shocked at my confession.

"Figured you would," she responds, not looking at me, her gaze trained on the pages in front of her.

I lean forward, my elbows on my knees. "You did?"

She nods.

"How would you even know about her anyway?"

This time she does look at me like I'm stupid. "Callan, we've been here for six months. There's only one woman you've had your eye on. You may try to be subtle, but I've known you your whole life," she says.

Dropping her socked feet to the floor, she rises and pads into the kitchen, leaving me frowning at her words. Have I been obvious? If Cayleigh's noticed, then others probably have as well.

"You know," Leigh says as she returns to the living room carrying a chilled bottle of beer, handing it to me. She perches her ass on the edge of the sofa and sips her tea. "It's been far too long since you've had a normal life. We've come here for that, to be normal. Give—"

"I'll never be normal, Leigh," I bite out in frustration. I gulp down the cold liquid, reveling in the burn of the bubbles as they make their way down my throat.

"Perhaps you don't want to let yourself be," she retorts.

Even though she's younger than me, she's got a good head on her shoulders. Being the only girl in the family, she's had it easier than Carrick and me. We were pulled into the business as soon as we could hold a gun. Cayleigh was Dad's baby girl. She was kept safe, on a pedestal, until she got caught up in the life when she got engaged to Niall.

For as long as I can remember, our father kept her hidden from the violence, and on her wedding day, she watched the man she loved get gunned down. His blood splattered on her white dress, on her pretty made-up face. And I couldn't do shit to help her, to save him.

I think the guilt of that will forever hang over me and Rick. Our lives were torn apart that day. But slowly we've found solace in each other. Now that Carrick has his woman, I see he's finally moving forward in life. I wish the same for Leigh.

For me, however, I don't see how it's possible. I'm the last remaining O'Leary, and our father will never just let me walk out of that life.

"Callan." My sister's voice drags me from the dark thoughts that seem to consume me. "If she's that special, you deserve to try." The problem with my sister is she still believes in love and happiness. She still holds on to those fucking fairy tales she reads.

"She's just a woman I fucked, Leigh. You read far too much into it." When she goes quiet again, I sigh, running my fingers through my hair. I want Madison, and I've already taken her. I've promised her security and orgasms. That's what a woman needs.

Don't get me wrong. I'll fuck any willing cunt, married or not, but walking away from Madison tonight has left me unsure. I don't think she's anything like her father. She's so much more. There's goodness in her; it drips from her pores, and I know I can't hurt her like I planned to.

I may bruise her and mark her physically, but that's what she wants. I'll give her the solace for the time I'm working for Magnus. But once I walk away, once this contract is over, I'll say goodbye.

"I'm going to bed." I finish my drink and head into one of the bedrooms. I should drive home, but I've been drinking, and I'm far too tired to focus.

I fall onto the mattress without taking off any clothes and shut my eyes for a moment, inhaling a breath only for my nostrils to be assaulted by her sweetness. Jesus, being around her is going to be difficult.

I pull my phone from my pocket and find her number. Hitting dial, I wait as I listen to each ring. I need to make sure she got home safely.

"You calling to apologize?" Her question has me chuckling, thinking about the asshole I was to her. Giving her shit for what she did to herself.

"Don't go looking for something that isn't there, Blossom. I don't apologize for shit I do," I respond easily, picturing her smiling as she sits in her bedroom.

"I figured that would be your answer," she says.

"I'm guessing you're home safely then."

"I am." Her confirmation settles the tension in my muscles.

Tomorrow I'll be a fucking chauffeur for her, making sure the pretty girl is safe wherever she goes. Her father made it very clear he wants his princess safe.

The contract has burned a hole in my hand, but it's signed. Accepted. I've become a bodyguard to a girl I want to fuck more than anyone I've ever met. Even though it's forbidden for me to even touch her, I've broken all the fucking rules.

"Go to bed now, and don't touch that little cunt

tonight," I warn her. "All your orgasms, every little whimper and moan are mine for the month. Do you understand me?"

"Yes, Callan," she purrs. She knows what she does to me. What she does to any man who walks into her world. "I didn't think you'd call."

"I didn't think you'd answer," I respond, staring up at the ceiling, trying to focus on something other than my cock fighting my zipper at the memory of her touch.

"I just wanted to thank you. Sins is the only place I feel safe since there's so much security there," she confesses in the dark. I wonder if she's lying on her bed. Is she naked? Fuck.

"You're no longer going to go to Sins," I inform her. Knowing my brother's not happy about my new job, I don't want to start shit in his club. If a man comes near Madison, I'll fucking gut the fucker.

"What? Why?" I picture her now, jolting up, her face creased in confusion.

"I don't approve. Those men—"

"*You don't approve?*" Her incredulous words have me sitting up, my back straight, my shoulders tense. "I like being there. I enjoy feeling wanted, and—" She wants to feel wanted? I'll fucking show her *wanted*.

"This isn't a fucking discussion, Madison. I'm in charge of keeping you safe, and if I say—"

"You're not my father. Do not speak to me like I'm a child."

Chuckling, I run my fingers through my unruly hair. "You are a child, Blossom. You're mine, Madison."

"I'm not yours to own. You made that clear, and I need it," she retorts hotly. Her voice laced with anger and frustration, but it's her confession that has my cock throbbing painfully.

"What does that mean?"

"I-I mean . . ." She sighs into the speaker, which doesn't help my aching body. "I want more."

"Jesus, Madison," I growl into the phone. Shutting my eyes so tight I see white behind the lids. The thought of this girl doing anything sinful doesn't help my reaction to her. I want to be the one leading her down an illicit path of debauchery. I need to be the one who she allows inside that sweet, tight little hole.

"It's the only thing that makes me feel. And . . . I

enjoyed it."

"You want me to hurt you again?" I question, my accent thicker and angrier than it was only moments ago.

"Yes," she whispers shyly, dropping her voice low, which only serves to make her even sexier.

Rearing my hand back, I slam it into the nightstand. Frustration ebbs and flows through me. Sexual frustration is something I can't deal well with. I need to fuck. I need that cunt tight around my dick.

"Are you okay? What was that?"

"You're making me fucking crazy, Blossom," I bite out. My teeth are clenched so hard my jaw aches. All the things I want to do to her right now race through my mind. Images of her bent over, legs spread wide. Skin flushed and pink.

"I like making you crazy." I can hear the smile in her voice. That she does. There's no lie there because it seems everything this girl does makes me want her more.

"You should be careful who you tease, Madison. Men don't like to be teased by little girls."

"And what, Callan" — she breathes my name seductively — "would you do if you were here right now?" There's a whimper right after she utters the last word that snaps all my fucking control. I have no morals, and I've never been ashamed. Pleasures of the body is something I never deny myself.

Shoving my zipper down, I tug at my jeans to get my cock out. The shaft is hot, hard, and ready for a sweet pussy or warm mouth, but my fist will have to do.

"Tell me what you'd want if I were there right now. I want to hear how you want to be fucked." It's an order. One I know she can't deny telling me.

"Well . . . uhm, I want you to bend me over the bed, or sofa, anywhere really," she begins.

Closing my eyes, I picture her with that pert little ass sticking up in the air.

"Then I want you to rip my panties down." Her voice gets husky, and I realize she's probably touching herself. The image causes arousal to drip from my shaft.

"And spank you?" I grit out.

"Yes, ten times. Five on each side," she says softly.

"Is that pretty pussy wet for me?"

"It is."

"Tell me how you lost your virginity," I murmur,

wanting to know about the time a man took that special part of her. The part I realize I would have loved to steal. To own.

"I was seventeen. He was a boy in my class."

"Did your pretty crimson virtue paint his cock, Blossom?" My voice is thick with desire, hunger for her.

"Yes." One word is merely a breath over the line, which makes my hand move up and down my cock faster and faster. I feel my release racing down my spine, the sensation almost euphoric.

"I wish I was the one to take it, to deflower the pretty blossom. To make you bleed on my cock, drenching me in your crimson innocence," I tell her, earning me a whimper and moan. She's no longer talking, and I know for a fact she's joining me in the pleasure that's taken ahold of me. "I would've pinned you to your pretty princess bed, told you that you're mine. And no other cock will be allowed near you. Then," I bite out as my hand tightens around my dick. "I'd make you scream while I stole your perfection. I'd make you fucking beg for more pain, more pleasure, more of my cock."

"Oh," is her response, and then she's breathing

raggedly.

"And you will be mine," I promise as my release shoots from the tip of my shaft spraying my stomach with sticky white cum. "I should stay so far away from you," I tell her with my hand still gripping my cock.

"Don't."

It's a plea. One that rips right through the commitment I made to her father. *Keep her safe.* Because I know that being with me will never allow her to be safe. I'm the monster wanting to steal the princess from her castle.

"You don't know what you're asking me for, Blossom," I utter, reaching for the box of Kleenex, which is sitting on the side table. With one hand, I clean myself up, and then head into the kitchen. I need a drink. Something strong.

"Yes, I do. Perhaps it's you who needs to let go for once."

"If I let go with you, I'm never going to stop."

It's a warning. I need her to stop taunting me because I'm a man who only has so much restraint. She's already snapped most of it, and I'm certain that once the final thread is broken, she'll never be the same again.

"Then don't stop. I'm asking you not to, and if I feel like I can't take it, I have a safe word. You told me so. I'm begging you to finally make me feel something," she pleads with me earnestly, and I wonder if I can really give this girl what she wants and needs.

"I can never love you." My response is confident. It's the truth. There's no way I can offer her something a girl like her was born for — a beautiful house, two-point-four kids, and a fucking white picket fence.

That's not who I am.

"I never asked you to love me." She's adamant. Stubborn and beautiful.

"You're a fucking temptation, Blossom. Are you ready to deal with your Daddy's wrath? I'm not the man he'd want for you," I tell her.

"Then he doesn't need to know. I'm an adult. Surely you can respect that?" She has a point. I should do right by her, but as always, I'm a selfish, arrogant bastard.

"Fine. As long as your little boyfriend stays out of my way."

I play my last straw. One final try before this girl is

mine.

"We're not together. I'll get you proof in the morning." She doesn't wait for my response. Instead, she hangs up, leaving me staring out the window into the dark night. She's just completely fucked me over, topping me from the bottom, and I have no idea how to take it from here.

Most women I've been with have been airheads. Ready for a fuck-and-chuck. But Madison Parker is different. She's so much more, and I don't think one taste will ever be enough.

Groaning, I pull a beer from the fridge and open the cap. I take a long swig, reveling in the cool liquid, but it does nothing to calm my boiling blood. I'm fueled not by anger, but desire. Hunger for my new little flower.

TEN

MADISON

The moon hangs low in the dark sky as I stare out my window. I'm not sure what I'm doing with Callan, but I can't not be with him. The sexual tension between us is palpable. I know I shouldn't even think about him, but my mind and body have other ideas.

My body still aches from being with him. Feeling him inside me. Each time I think about it, my core pulses wildly, needing the roughness he offered. I'd never felt so good yet so emotional before. The intensity of a scene was always something that scared me. I thought that perhaps being so close to someone, having them see your innermost needs and wants would hurt me emotionally, but it's only given me more confidence.

There's a strength in allowing someone to control

you, to trust someone so implicitly with not only your body but your soul. It's daunting, but beautiful.

Picking up my phone, I glance at the time. Five in the morning. Swiping over the screen to unlock the device, I scroll through Facebook, Instagram, but nothing keeps my interest. Nothing, because Callan isn't on social media.

I suppose his job doesn't allow time for friends.

Or *girlfriends*.

The thought slams into my chest, causing an ache to form where my heart thuds violently against my ribs. I'm jealous of a man who has blatantly told me that we'll be fuck buddies, nothing more.

The bed covers feel heavy as frustration burns its way through my veins. I'm not a teenage girl who has a crush on the hottest boy in school. *So why does it feel like I am?*

Rising from the bed, I pad over to the patio door, pulling it open to inhale the fresh, early morning air. The gentle wind billows through the gap, licking at my skin, causing goose bumps to rise on every inch of my flesh.

The sun is peeking through the clouds, a gentle

glimpse of gold and orange between a rather gloomy sky, and I wonder if today holds any more revelations than yesterday did.

Will Callan actually admit to caring for me?

Heading back inside, I pull off my skimpy nightdress and head into the bathroom attached to my bedroom. The spacious area is tiled with the most expensive designs from Italy, with ornate silver taps and glass imported from somewhere in London. Everything in this house screams money.

It's opulence I find wasteful. I always have.

I'm a simple girl, living in a world that's far too lavish for me. And that's why I hide from the paparazzi. I don't want to do the interviews Daddy schedules for me. But I do it because I love him.

As much as he rules my life in many ways, he's also had to be pulled in three directions all my life. He's had to be mother, father, as well as Senator. A man living in the public eye. And I have to be honest, I haven't been the easiest daughter.

I lather my skin with the orange-scented body wash, the citrus smell mixed with a gentle hint of flowers makes it my favorite. It reminds me of my mother, how she would always smell of freshly cut flowers and the orange juice she'd squeeze for breakfast, that was long before she'd become a woman obsessed with money. When she was someone more loving than the cold-hearted bitch she'd turned into later in my life. And then she left.

Even in the spray of the water cascading down my body, tears trickle down my cheeks. I recall the day she left. When she walked out and never looked back. Since that day to this one, I felt it like a missing piece of who I am. My life had changed once more when my father became Senator, and I was thrown into a role I didn't want.

I rinse off, reminding myself I'm lucky I have a home, a roof over my head, and the opportunities other children haven't had. My father, on the other hand, he's taken on more than he could've thought possible, and as the years passed, I saw him change. I watched as he became a man I no longer recognize.

The exhaustion of a sleepless night grips me tight in its hold, but I couldn't sleep. I'm hyped up, so perhaps breakfast and a coffee will help. I have things to do today, and hopefully I don't fall asleep during the meeting scheduled with a local charity.

Stepping out of the shower with my mind still on the past, I glance up to find a figure in my bathroom. A scream falls from my lips as I'm met with the dark eyes of Callan O'Leary.

"What the fu—"

"Morning, Blossom," he smirks while allowing his heated gaze to hungrily trail over my naked, wet frame. He holds out a towel, which I snatch and wrap around me, but it's pointless. He's seen everything.

"Why are you here, in my room?" I hiss, pushing by him, making my way back into my bedroom.

"I work for you. Or did you forget that little tidbit of information?" He settles himself against the doorjamb of my bathroom, watching me move into the closet. I pull out a pair of jeans and white, fitted T-shirt, along with underwear I pull on before heading back into the bedroom. I don't know why I'm hiding from him, but in the light of day, it feels strange having him look at me.

"How could I forget?" I bite out in frustration.

Turning to him once more, I pin him with a glare, which only earns me a chuckle. "You're such an asshole."

"Are you going to tell me that every time you see me, baby girl?" he quips, amusement lacing his tone.

"Yes."

"Let's just forget you feel that way," he says, stalking toward me.

I step back, keeping my gaze on his. He stops inches from me. His large frame dwarfing me as he leans in. His mouth is so close to mine I can almost taste the bitter coffee on his warm breath.

"Those are such a pretty pair of tits. Does your boyfriend know how to tease them until you're coming all over his dick like I can?" He doesn't wait for my answer. Turning on his heel, he leaves me gaping at the closed door to my bedroom.

"Asshole!" I call out, hoping he can hear me. I drop the towel, smothering myself in orange blossom moisturizer. I ensure I'm scented like a citrus field before getting dressed.

Twenty minutes later, I make my way down the hall, noticing the sun is already high in the clear, blue sky.

The number of windows and glass in our home makes it difficult to remain in the dark at times. The one thing I remember about my mother was her love of our old house. It was small, nothing like this place at all. A low-key home, with an old-style fireplace, almost like those old English manor houses. But as soon as we moved in here, she changed. Dad wanted to have an ostentatious place to host his dinner parties, and she decided to leave.

"There's the princess." A thick Irish accent comes from behind me.

I turn to find Callan staring at me with a grin on his handsome face. His eyes are crinkled at the corners as he watches me with amusement.

"You seem to be making yourself at home," I remark, stalking by him to find my glass of orange juice sitting on the counter beside a plate of toast in the kitchen.

"Well, for the next four weeks, this will be my home," he tells me, causing me to whip around on my heel and meet his stare.

"What do you mean?"

"I'll be here every day and every night, Blossom. Your Daddy is off on a trip to Washington, and I'll be here to watch over his little girl." He seems far too excited to be telling me. My father didn't mention that he'd be gone for so long. And neither did Hudson.

"You're not living in the same house as I am. We may have had one scene in the club, but you're not my babysitter. I can take care of myself."

He doesn't seem perturbed by my order, but he should be because I will not sleep under the same roof as Callan. Especially when he knows how to make my toes curl and my body respond in ways I've never felt before. It's not safe. The closer he is, the more I'll want him, and if that happens, I'll feel more than I should. More than we agreed on.

"I'm serious," I inform him, gulping down my juice as I watch him.

He closes the distance between the counter where I'm standing and himself. When he reaches it, he ignores me by not offering a response. Instead, he butters my toast and places grated cheese from a container on the bread. Shifting the plate over toward me, he glances my way.

"Eat. We're leaving in ten minutes."

He turns to walk out of the kitchen, and as much as I want to refuse him, I know the next time I'll get a chance to have anything to eat will be for my late lunch with the women's charity in town.

I quickly eat my breakfast, with my coffee still steaming beside my plate. I hate rushing, but it seems the sooner we're on our way, the sooner I can get him off my back for a few hours. I know I'll spend the day bored, thinking about him and what happened between us, but the farther away he is from me, the better.

At least that will keep me safe. There's something about the way my mind convinces me that jumping him is a good idea. This is purely sex. Nothing more. But it's when he offers me that cocky smirk that pushes me far over the limit. I can't help myself when I'm around him, and I know it's not that he can hurt me psychically that scares me. It's that he can hurt me emotionally.

It's been a long week of being driven around by the man I want. He hasn't touched me again, but there's been tension between us. So palpable that you could cut it with a knife.

With meetings upon meetings to ensure the charities that are in need get the funding my father's office promised them, there's not been enough time for us to talk properly, and in the evenings, he heads to Sins, where he's banned me from going. So, I've put on my professionalism like my father taught me, but deep down, it's not my choice to race around, writing checks.

Today though, I'm at the one place I want to be. A homeless shelter that speaks to my heart. Not some money-grabbing corporate, but a place where they're actually helping others.

"Madison, I think your father's team should set that up." A voice drags me from the daydream of the silent drive that brought me here.

"I'm sorry?"

"Are you listening to me, dear?" Mrs. Garforth stares at me like I have two heads. The old woman dressed in her Sunday best is the head of the charity that collects money for abused and abandoned babies in the city. Her work is something I believe in, the one charity my father has pushed on me that I respect.

"Yes, I'm sorry. Dad's away, and I've been busy with non-stop meetings to ensure all the charities are seen to. I'll make a note for the ladies to set that up. I'll have Theresa call you and make sure all the details are correct before sending out the press release," I tell her, earning me a happy smile.

The more money we can bring in, the more they can put toward the shelter, which in turn means they can help more children. Orphans who have no one to care for them.

"That's wonderful, dear," she coos, rising from her seat to indicate the meeting is over. "Thank you for taking the time to come and see us today. It's always so nice to have you here."

"You know it's a pleasure," I tell her, shoving my notebook, iPad, and pen back into the purse I carry to all meetings. When I stand, I find the door sliding open and Callan standing there dressed in a black suit and tie and a crisp, white shirt. He's changed. This morning, he was in a pair of jeans and a T-shirt that hugged his muscled arms and chest.

"Is that your gentleman?" the old lady gasps.

"No, no, just my driver," I tell her, hopefully not blushing in the process.

She casts another glance at him, then leans in to whisper conspiratorially in my ear, "Rather fetching for a driver, dear."

"He's far too old for me anyway," once again I assure her, but she's having none of it.

"You know, Harold and I are fifteen years apart. Granted, he is an old fogey now, but he was quite a gentleman in his day." She laughs. It's a soft sound that reminds me of my gran before she passed away. That calming sound that holds you in its warmth.

Affection.

It's not something I'm used to. Not even Hudson shows it. My father hasn't offered me any in years, so I've come to live without it. I grew up in a home where I'm meant to be strong. To be grown up before I could even fathom what was going on.

Even though my father made sure I was cared for, he wasn't loving. There weren't hugs and kisses. He may have made sure I got my bedtime stories and orange juice, but there was never an affectionate hug or cuddle.

When I fell and hurt my knee or scuffed my toe, I was told to breathe through the pain. So, I did. I breathed through losing all my family besides him.

"I'll see you next week," I tell the lady as tears sting my eyes.

"You go on; your man is waiting on you." She smiles, and I shake my head.

Making my way toward the door, Callan holds it open, allowing me to exit. He follows me down the steps and out into the warm afternoon.

"How was your meeting?" he questions, opening the back door of the SUV for me.

"Boring. They need more money, and I have to come up with it somewhere."

He watches me for a moment before nodding and shutting the door. He rounds the front of the vehicle and slips into the driver's seat.

"Why don't you let me sit up front with you?" I question.

He stops all movement. Glancing in the rearview mirror, he lifts his mouth into a sinful smirk. "Because I'd be distracted by your pretty legs, picturing them around my neck while I ate your sweet cunt. So, it's best you sit back there." He turns on the radio loud, and Linkin Park sings "Numb" so loud I can't respond to his filthy words.

ELEVEN

CALLAN

I focus on the music as I weave through traffic. I spent the day in her father's office, finding the documents Oliver needed. Once that was out of the way, I wondered how I was going to get through the next few weeks babysitting a woman I hunger to fuck violently.

My life has been spent in the most expensive homes in London, sometimes undercover, other times not. But for the most part, all my marks were assholes, men with too much money. Or men with secrets that needed to be exposed, one way or another.

I've used methods of torture that would make anyone squirm. And right now, all I can think about is her. I took it upon myself to make sure the staff knew they could take some time off tonight so I can be near her. I ensured the house is secure, especially with me at Sins while she's here alone. Even though Hudson is still lurking around the city, and no doubt he'll most probably want to visit his girlfriend later, I know as soon as he leaves, I'll have her all to myself.

I don't know why I did it. There's no point in torturing myself, but I do. Being inside her was like heaven. It awakened emotions in me that were dormant for so long. And now, all I can think of is her taking my cock, my punishments again.

She proved it when she unraveled on the phone with me. When I heard her soft moans and sweet whimpers, I was a goner. But she also took all I wanted to give her in the scene we played out. It was like a dream. A woman who's my equal, who can experience pleasure from the darker delights this world offers.

When her father called me to let me know he needed to go away for some time and needed me on-site, I agreed quickly. There was no way I would allow her to stay in the house alone. Something tells me she would prefer it that way, but not everything she wants will be handed to her on a silver platter. Me included.

It's no secret we fit, but the thing that worries me is her youth. She could allow emotions to cloud her judgment, and that's what I should be concerned about. Other than that, I know her safety is in my hands, and there's nothing I won't do to ensure that.

Oliver needs to get back to me to confirm everything I sent him was legit. That he didn't need any more to take her father down.

The only problem is her boyfriend. He's one I want to take down as well. That little prick better steer very far from me, or I'll make sure his cock gets cut off and shoved up his arse. Perhaps if he walked in while I was balls-deep in his girlfriend, it would cement the fact that she doesn't want him. At least, it will confirm she wants a man, not a boy.

"Are you going to talk to me?" she questions from the backseat as I turn toward their house. I cast a quick glance in the mirror but don't answer. I allow her to stew for a few more moments, but I know her, and I know she won't stop until I do. We're pulling into the driveway when she finally cracks and continues her tirade. "This is ridiculous, Callan. If you're going to be—"

"Madison, get out of the car," I finally respond, turning to glance over my shoulder at her.

Her mouth falls open in shock at my harsh tone, but I don't apologize. *Why should I?* She's convinced I'm an arsehole, so that's what I'll give her. She stares at me indignantly, and I half expect her to fight back, but she doesn't.

Shoving the door open, she exits the SUV, and I'm finally able to breathe. I don't know what this woman is doing to me, but it's not something I'm used to. I should've listened to Rick. When he told me to walk away, at least, to not pursue her, I should've taken his advice. But I'm stubborn, and now I'm here with no way out. The only thing is, I don't want a way out.

I watch her pert little ass as she makes her way inside, leaving me to calm my hard-on before following her into the house. Shutting the front door, I wander through the foyer and find her in the kitchen, pouring herself a glass of orange juice.

"Sometimes, you need to learn that silence is as powerful as any words you can throw at someone, Blossom," I tell her, stalking closer to the woman who has me wrapped around her finger.

Her breathing hitches when I take her glass, lifting it to my lips and taking a sip of the cold liquid. I lean in. Grasping her chin, I tilt her head toward me. Our mouths fuse for a moment as I trickle the sweet juice into her mouth.

It's an intimate gesture, one I haven't done in years. One that I haven't *wanted* to do. When I've fed her everything, I plant a soft kiss on her full lips, reveling in the taste of her. There's something so sweet about this woman.

She swallows, her heartbeat erratic as it pulses along her slender, delicate neck. The smooth, creamy flesh just begs to be marked. When I walked in on her last week and found her in all her naked glory, it took all my restraint not to pin her against the tiles and fuck her senseless.

"Do you enjoy giving me whiplash? You know, women are meant to be the indecisive ones," she murmurs.

Her big, brown eyes meet mine. Questions dance in them, begging and pleading for more. She wants to learn about me, about the darkness that lurks within me. *Would she run when she learned what I'm really like?* I've done so many things she can never know about.

"It's not being indecisive, Blossom," I smirk, watching her eyes shimmer as they try to probe mine for all the answers to who I am. "It's called being cautious. Because I grew up knowing it was either be an arsehole or get killed. So, in my defense, I wanted to live."

She shakes her head, placing her small hands on my chest, searing me with the gentlest touch. My body is tense, taut in an attempt to reign in my need to push her against the kitchen counter and spread her legs. I want to open her, to delve into her depths, inside her mind, inside her body. Fuck, I need it.

"And now that you're living? Is there any reason you're still so angry?" Her question is harmless, but it slams right into my chest, burrowing a gaping wound wide open. With mere words, she's floored me. Gripped my heart in her small hand, and she's squeezing.

She's stealing all my fucking breath, and I'm fucked because I want to give it all to her. I want to inhale her, devour her, to feast on her body until there's nothing left. I want to make her feel the wrath I've held onto for so long I've kept it within me because it's allowed me to live, to kill when I needed to without guilt.

"Yes, there is."

"What is it?" she questions, her body far too close to mine, her mouth only inches from where I can devour it with my own. I want to steal every breath she takes and swallow every sound she makes.

"I want something that will land me in a shit-load of trouble, but I can't find it within me to stop myself from taking it. Usually, I wouldn't give a fuck. I'd plough through your world and leave it in shambles." My confession causes her breath to hitch once more. She swallows loudly, her tongue darting out to wet her lips, leaving them glossed in her saliva. "But you've fucked with me, baby girl." My eyes are glued to her face, her neck, her cleavage. The air is heavy with desire, that innate need for each other.

"And what if that thing you want just offers itself to you without qualms? If it assures you that nothing bad will happen to you?" There's a hint of a smile on her lips as she says this.

My mouth kicks into a grin at her question. "If I took it, there's no way it will ever survive the onslaught I have planned."

This time she giggles at my confession. My hands reach for her hips, holding her steady as I walk her backward against the marble counter. Lifting her easily, I plant her ass on the top. She squeaks when her body makes contact with mine as I shuffle between her open thighs.

"If I took it," I continue, "there's no telling what the outcome would be. Perhaps I'll break it. Make it quiver and pulse. Make it wet and needy."

"I don't see anything wrong with that," she rasps, and I know she's as turned on as I am. I want to lean in, I want to steal her mouth, but before I can, the front door flies open, and I hear his voice before we see him.

"Madison," Hudson calls to her, causing me to step back. It's as if a cold bucket of water was just chucked at me, and I release my hold on her. The thick neediness that hung in the air evaporates, and our moment is gone.

She hops off the counter, stalking toward me. Then she leans up on her tip-toes and whispers in my ear, "I hope that you take it soon. I wish for you to break it, to have your wicked way with it. Remember, Hudson and I aren't together. I wish you'd believe me."

With that, she leaves me in the kitchen staring out the large bay window at the garden beyond. Then I hear her greet him.

"Hey. What are you doing here?"

"I came to see you, babe," he says. I hear the smile in his words.

"Hudson, he's not here. You don't have to keep up the pretense." Her voice is filled with frustration, and I wonder if she's doing it for me, or if they really are just a smokescreen for her father. I know he wants his precious princess to be with the white knight, but she's definitely got a thing for the bad boy in this story.

I head out toward the pool house where I'm staying for the time Mr. Parker is away. He offered me a room in the house, but there's just too much temptation. I know if I walk in on her while she's a sleepy mess in those tiny pink shorts, there's no way they'll survive.

They'd be ripped from her slim hips and on the floor in seconds. And I'd have my mouth on her sweet cunt devouring every inch of her. My cock aches as I flop onto the bed. Staring up at the ceiling, I breathe through the desire coursing through my veins. My blood is heated for her.

This will definitely be the most difficult job I've ever had. But when I think of her, I know I'd do anything to keep her safe. Even from myself.

TWELVE

MADISON

Pushing my bedroom door open, I'm too aware Callan's been inside here, seen me naked. Hudson is hot on my heels as I set my purse on the bed and turn to him. He looks ever the prep-school boy, dressed in an expensive suit. His hair is perfectly styled, his smooth, square jaw free of any stubble. In other words, completely opposite of Callan.

"I've missed you," he tells me, leaning in to steal a kiss, but I turn my face away, causing his lips to brush my cheek in a swipe of heat. "What's wrong, Madicakes?" He's called me that all the time I've known him. At first, I thought it was cute, but right now, it sends a shudder of revulsion through me.

I realize in that moment I can't pretend to play this

game anymore. He's been wanting me to lie about us to my father so he can further his career when I know for a fact he's out sleeping with every girl who falls into his Aston Martin.

But it's time to set the record straight. Lying isn't getting me anywhere. And I can't do it anymore. Not to my father and certainly not to Hudson.

"I'm just tired of this song and dance, Hudson. My father isn't here. You don't have to pretend we're together. This"— I gesture between us — "I can't do it anymore."

"What are you talking about?" he sneers, gripping my arms, his fingers digging into the sensitive skin. I've never seen him angry. But his face right now is an image of rage. There's fire burning in his blue eyes.

"Hudson, let me go. You're hurting me," I beg. My voice is a whimper.

He's taller than me. Bigger, bulkier, and there's no way I can pull free from his hold.

"Listen to me, Madi. I don't give a shit if your father isn't home. You've been playing the little slut down at that club for months, and I haven't told him," he hisses with venom dripping from every word. "Did you want your precious daddy to find out what you do down there?"

"I don't know what you're talking about," I tell him, hoping he'll release me, but he doesn't. Instead, he shakes me back and forth, his hot breath on my face.

"Don't lie to me. I've had you followed for months. I'm not stupid, Madicakes. You play the angel for your father, but you're nothing but a slut spreading your legs for men when you don't even want to kiss me." His words crack my resolve, and I claw at his hands, my nails digging into the flesh.

"Let. Me. Go." I enunciate each word carefully, hoping it doesn't set him off, but I'm wrong when he releases one arm. His hand rears back and makes contact with my face, causing me to cry out in pain.

The sting on my cheek, the tears that pool in my eyes are enough to confirm this wasn't the best idea. I should've told him downstairs. At least I know Callan is down there, and he could've stopped this.

I spin on my heel, the one thing I recall from self-defense classes; but Hudson is too fast and grabs my ankle, tugging my leg until I'm unbalanced, and I find myself falling to my knees. My hands hit the carpet, and he chuckles behind me.

"Or what? You going to run to the bodyguard you're fucking?" He leans in, grunting angrily, spittle flying from his mouth landing on my face.

"Please, Hudson. What the fuck has gotten into you?" I turn, kicking at his knee, which has him growling in response.

"Fucking bitch," he snarls angrily. "You think you can play coy? I know what's going on here. I'm not stupid." His voice is cold, harsh, and I'm still jarred by his change in demeanor. He wasn't always a nice guy, but this is something entirely different.

"Hudson, please—"

"Shut up!" he hisses. "Does daddy know you're whoring your precious cunt to the bodyguard?" My mouth falls open, but no words come out. "I thought so." This time, his laugh is demented.

Another harsh slap on my cheek, and I can't hold back the tears anymore. I blink, causing his image to blur in front of me. He rears his hand back once more, and I flinch, awaiting the impact, but it never comes.

When I open my eyes, I find Callan straddling Hudson, his fists making crunching sounds against Hudson's nose, jaw, and before he punches his throat, I'm pulling him away. I don't know where my strength comes from, or how I manage to snap Callan from his rage, but I do.

"Just let him go."

"Listen to me, you little fucker. I have boys like you for breakfast. If you ever"— he leans in, spit flying from his lips in rage — "ever come near Madison again, I'll make sure you're sorry for fucking being born." The tone of his voice scares me, and I'm the one he's defending. I'm not sure what's going on. Something must have set Hudson off, but the only thing I can think of right now is the pain in my jaw.

"This isn't the end. Her father will hear about this," comes the final threat from a man I grew up knowing. But as I watch him walk out of my bedroom, he's a stranger to me.

Callan turns to me. Meeting my watering gaze, he cups my face in his hands. His thumbs, rough and calloused, swipe the tears from my cheeks. "If he comes near you again, I will fucking kill him."

"You didn't—"

"I'm paid to care for you, to keep you safe, but even if I wasn't being paid, I'd fucking do it in a heartbeat." His words hold a seriousness that steals my breath.

"You're paid to care for me?" I question, watching him for a flinch of emotion. Anything. Just a sign to tell me he's here, that he feels what I do.

I'm not going crazy. I can't be.

I watch as he stares at me. His eyes boring into mine, as if he's searching for answers to questions he's not voiced yet. My stinging face held gently in his hands.

"If I was just another girl, and you weren't being paid, would you have saved me as well?" I wince at how weak I sound. Like a little girl looking for a fairytale prince. But the man before me is not that. He's bad. He told me so himself.

"Blossom, I would save you any time, any place, from any one. It's in my nature to protect, but it's also in my nature to kill, maim, torture."

I pull away from him. Stepping back, I take him in

fully. His shirt is dotted with Hudson's blood, his hands stained in crimson. This is him. The wild beast. The untamed gentleman. A contrast. Even dressed in a suit, he'll never be a man my father would allow me to be with.

The thought lances my chest. My heart aches. As much as I want Callan and he wants me, even with Hudson out of the way, I know Senator Parker would never allow his little girl to date "the help" as he calls all the people who work for him.

"All the times you tell me you're so bad, I don't see it, Callan."

"You should, little flower. Because I'll steal all your pretty petals. I'll rip them off one by one until you're merely a stem between my fingers. And I'll do it because I want to be the only person to break you, and the only one who can keep you safe."

"What if I no longer have any petals? What if I have thorns?" I question, finding confidence from deep within me. I meet his darkened stare. The way he watches me is like a predator about to hunt his prey. But there's no chase, because I give myself to him willingly.

Something about this man makes me crazy. I don't care what Daddy says. I no longer care what the paparazzi or the press make of me or my choices. I want this man before me.

"Then I best be careful when I touch you," he murmurs. Stalking toward me, he closes the distance in a few easy steps. The heat emanating from him sears me, leaving me breathless, needy, and aching for him to ravage me.

"Don't be careful with me. I'm not a delicate flower. Show me what you want to do to me," I implore him in a raspy whisper. My face still hurts, the agony from Hudson's harsh blows still smart my jaw, but I want this so much more.

"Jesus, Madison," he growls, gripping my hips and pulling me closer. He leans in, his lips on mine in an instant. I gasp in shock at the electric current jolting through me. Every nerve in my body is alive as his tongue dips into my mouth, licking at me, tasting me.

I deepen the kiss. My arms snake around his neck, pulling him closer, pressing my body against his as if I need to be near him to stay alive. His hands trail down to my ass, grasping me and lifting me.

My legs wrap around his waist as he walks us toward the wall, where he slams my back against the cool surface. His lips move south, latching onto my neck, suckling the flesh into his mouth. A gentle graze of his teeth draws a whimper from my mouth as I tangle my fingers in his short hair.

I want more, so much more, but he stops in an instant. Pulling away, he meets my hungry gaze. "We can't do this now. I can't . . ." His words trail off, and I wonder what's turned him from hot and heavy to ice cold.

He sets me down, then moves away from me. I watch as he makes his way to the balcony door. Ensuring it's locked, he flits his gaze over to where I'm still leaning against the wall.

"I'll be in the pool house if you need me."

Quietly, he opens the door and leaves me reeling from being attacked both violently and passionately. Sighing, I push off the wall and pad into the bathroom to open the taps and splash my face with cold water.

With a quick glance in the mirror, I find my eyes

bloodshot from the tears and my cheek bright red from Hudson's assault. I don't know what got into him. He's never once touched me in that way. For years, I thought I knew him, but it turns out even time can change someone.

When I head back into my bedroom, I find my phone and tap out a message to Amber telling her to call me as soon as she can. I don't know if Hudson would go to her for anything, but I have a feeling after the fight we just had, he'll be trying to ensure I'm the one who's thrown in the deep end if this blows up in our faces.

All the time I've been going to Sins, I've never once been with any of the men in the club. None of them held my attention enough. Then Callan walked in, and I continued to go, to see him.

Now, all I need is for him to trust me and show me who he really is. Tugging off my black slacks, I replace them with a pair of cotton shorts. The top I'm wearing finds its place on the carpet, and I pull on a loose-fitting T-shirt. It's casual and sexy, but not too revealing.

My face is smarting, so I make my way down to the kitchen to grab some ice. When I walk into the space, I find Callan at the kitchen table, his nose buried in his phone, and I wonder who he's texting. It's ridiculous. I feel like a jealous girlfriend. Shaking my head, I open the fridge and pull out the small ice pack I use after running. Wrapping it in a tea towel, I place it on my cheek and can't stop the moan of relief that falls from my lips.

"If you keep making those goddamn sounds, Blossom, I'm not going to get any work done," he says from behind me.

I turn to look at him. He's pulled open a laptop and is tapping away. I make my way to him, still holding the ice-cold pack to my face and settle on the chair opposite him. He doesn't look at me. Instead, he carries on typing. His brow creased in concentration as his dark eyes are pinned to the screen.

I sit back, my gaze never straying from him. He's handsome. Rugged and rough around the edges. He's no longer wearing the blood-splattered shirt but a blue tee that seems to be molded to his frame. His muscles bulge with movement as he works. And the sprawling veins that adorn his arms make me want to trace the intricate patterns with my tongue. I want to see more.

So much more.

Show me what you hide, Callan, please.

.

THIRTEEN

CALLAN

"Do you really care?" she questions, causing my fingers to freeze midair. There's nothing humorous about her words. And I realize with each day I'm around her, I want her more. My first week of work was just that. With her in meetings, I didn't make a move. I allowed her to be the professional I've come to learn she is, but she's slowly burrowing her way under my skin.

And I decide to give her an honest answer, so I nod. "I do."

"Why?" Once again, she pushes for more. I wanted this to be nothing more than a job, but I can't deny it's becoming more.

"I've always been professional when it comes to jobs, Madison," I inform her. The words are raspy, and

I can hear the emotion in my tone. She's heard it too. Raking my fingers through my hair, I lift my eyes to meet hers. "I've never allowed myself to have what my brother does, what normal people do."

Her face is a picture of sadness. There's affection in her expression, which jolts my heart once more. Each time she looks at me like that it forces me to wonder. To play with the idea of having a woman beside me.

"What if you can have it all?" she asks with a gentle smile, lifting one perfectly sculpted eyebrow in question. "I mean, maybe since you've been in *that* life for so long, you allowed yourself to be immersed in it. But here" — she gestures between us — "you don't need to be that person anymore. You came here for a new life. Didn't you?"

"I did," I agree. My answer earns me a megawatt smile.

"Then take me out. Let's do something together," she implores. "I'm done needing a babysitter. Be something else. I'm going to get dressed, and you're going to take me out." She giggles. The sound is beautiful, lighthearted, and it makes me smile in return.

I watch her spin on her heel and stalk from the kitchen.

I leave her be and finish up the work I had, but my mind is running rampant with ideas of where to take her. We have the gala event on Friday, and tomorrow I have to take her shopping with her so-called best friend, but today I vow to make it all about her.

I've never really dated anyone in a long while. It's not in my nature, but this girl makes me want that. All that bullshit. Granted, I'll never be one for romance, but I can certainly treat her to an afternoon of good food, and perhaps learn more about this beauty.

Her big brown eyes peek up at me from the opposite side of the table. The café we're in isn't busy, so we found a small booth in the back of the restaurant.

"What are you thinking?" she asks, watching me intently.

"About how beautiful you'd look sitting on this table with your pretty pussy open, ready for me to eat." Honesty earns me a blush. Dark lashes flutter against her cheeks as she drops her gaze.

"Do you always hide behind sex?" she breathes through her frustration, her chest rising and falling catching my stare.

"Not always, but you drive me to it," I retort playfully.

"Men seem to do that, hide behind emotionless words and actions." Her observation makes me angry. In the time we've spent together, I've offered her more affection than I have given anyone my whole life.

"I'm not your father," I bite out. The words are harsh, and I realize how that sounded.

"Fuck you, Callan."

"I didn't mean—"

She interrupts me with an observation that jars me for a moment. "If you spend your life angry at how it turned out, don't blame others. All I meant was you don't have to be cold with me. I want this. I want you. Is that so difficult to understand?"

"I'm not good at this," I tell her, waving my hand around. "Dating and all that bullshit your little prep-school boy gave you, that's not me."

"No, because you're a man, I get that. But you've given me more solace than he ever did." Her fire blazes through me, heating my blood with need for this woman.

"You mean those scars?"

She drops her head, fiddling with the tablecloth, the cup before her, anything else, but she doesn't look at me. "They were a buildup of years of pain, of being bullied by girls like Amber and boys like Hudson."

"What changed? You're best friends with her and you were dating him."

She shakes her head. "When I got to college, I lost weight. I focused on fitness, so I didn't have to go through what I did in school, but the damage was already done. After my mother left when I was twelve, I started," her voice raspy with the pain from years of anguish.

"Where is she now? Your mother."

A sad laugh falls from her lips at my question. "She died a long while ago. We got the news that she'd had a heart attack. I'm not sure on the details, but my father told me. I didn't feel a thing when I heard. I spent my life angry with her for leaving me to fend off the bullies. My father never cared."

Her words grip my heart. That cold, dead muscle that's been sleeping soundly for years is alive and beating for her. Only for her. It should scare the fuck out of me, but it doesn't. *I care about her.*

"Since we've been . . . I mean, since we've gotten to know each other, I haven't wanted to cut. I haven't felt that innate need to hurt myself."

If I didn't think I was falling for this girl before, I am now. And I know when she finally lifts those beautiful cinnamon eyes to mine, that she feels it too. It's flickering like a candle in the dark, and I'm the moth, ready to fly to my demise.

"I wanted to scare you away," I tell her. "I didn't want to corrupt you with my darkness, my anger, and yet—"

"Yet, I have my own demons," she tells me with a small smile. "I think you're the one who was scared." Her observation is correct. I was scared when I saw the goodness in her.

I can't help chuckling at her words. I've never been scared of anything my whole life. I've killed, tortured, and maimed men since I turned sixteen. Fear wasn't a factor in my mind. A wasted emotion, just like love. But she's right.

"I'm serious," Madison says. Her words are low, a mere whisper. "You were afraid of feeling something for me." She nods at her conclusion, and I can't fault her. There's no nervousness in this girl. Her body is rigid. Straight and confident. She's so sure of herself right now.

I wanted to break her, to make her scream and cry, while watching her pieces fall. But I realize she's already shattered. Slowly, she's taken each fragment and glued herself back together, and somehow, it's molded her into someone who fits into my broken parts.

She doesn't even know why I'm really here. I've veered off my path to take her down along with her father. She's not him. So far from it, and as the realization slowly dawns on me, I make it my mission to keep her safe from what's about to happen to her precious father. I'm going to give her anything she needs. I shouldn't do this, but I'm dying to see her cry. To watch those pretty brown eyes glisten with tears, but instead of sadness, they'll be tears of pleasure.

She rises, smiles down at me, then leans in. "I'll be

in the rest room if you want to follow."

I wait, listening to her footfalls disappear before I call for the check. Once it's paid, I'm out of my chair and following the path she took moments ago.

Shoving open the door to the ladies, I find one cubicle closed, but when the click of the lock sounds behind me, she steps out.

"I knew you couldn't resist." She smiles playfully. But the moment I'm closer, nearing her, the smile falls away, and I'm met with the heat in her pretty eyes. "Touch me, Callan," she purrs, her hand reaching for me.

Lightning fast, I grip both her wrists, binding them with my one hand behind her back as I shove us both into the cubicle and kick the door shut behind us. With my free hand, I reach into the tiny pair of shorts she's wearing for me. No doubt they are for me. I find her cotton panties soaked with her arousal.

"Is this what you wanted?" I press two fingers against her clit hard. Roughly. She gasps when I push the material into her tight hole. They drench in her slickness, and I smirk. "Your little cunt gets wet for this dangerous man?" I question, but I don't need her to answer. I know what she'll say. Shoving the material to the side, I stroke her smooth lips, finding a soft patch of hair on her mound. "A naughty little girl. Do you want to submit your beautiful body to me so I can have my wicked way with you? Do you want to hear what a bad man I am while I finger your tight, wet hole?"

She nods. I laugh. A wholehearted laugh.

I can't drag my eyes away from her, she's far too beautiful.

"Come for me, sweetheart," I coo in her ear as I tease her, stroking her, dipping my fingers into her heat. Her head drops back. She grips my shoulders, clawing at me as I finger-fuck her in a restroom.

She doesn't care. Her pearly white teeth bite down on her lower lip as she whimpers and mewls. And when her walls pulse around my fingers, I know she's about to unravel, and I can't turn away. My eyes locked on this beautiful creature who's mine. All fucking mine.

And as much as I wanted to push her away, I can't. I pull my fingers from her body. Bringing my fingers up to my nose, I inhale her scent. The juices on both digits glisten, and I can't stop myself from licking them clean.

"Thank you," she whispers, smiling like she's just been in heaven.

"Get cleaned up. I'll wait at the car for you." I lean in, planting a gentle kiss to her lips and leave her in the restroom.

When she joins me outside, her cheeks are still pink, and her eyes still shimmer with happiness. I open the door, allowing her to slip into the passenger seat. Once I'm beside her, I start the engine and pull out onto the road.

"What if I was dating Hudson when we had our first scene? Would you have still fucked me that night?" Her question makes me smile. It's innocent, genuinely so.

"I'm a man with very few morals, darling. If I want something, I take it," I inform her easily while keeping my eyes on the road. "If you were still with Hudson, I'd fuck your tight little cunt, fill it with my cum, then send you back to him so he could eat your pussy and taste me inside you."

Her gasp is the only response I get, so I leave it at that. We could continue this conversation back at the house later, but right now, I want to make sure she enjoys a normal day, or date, whichever way you look at it.

FOURTEEN

MADISON

It's been almost two weeks since Callan's been in my life. He's the only reason I frequented Seven Sins so much. I know his brother owns the club. Carrick is an enigma, and now that he's engaged to Peyton, he's even more wanted. I've overheard women talk about how they wanted to snag him up. They want what Peyton has, and as much as I agree that Carrick is handsome, it's his older brother who's stolen my attention.

"Good morning, Blossom." A deep rumble startles me from reading in the early morning sunshine streaming through my window.

When my eyes lift to the doorway, Callan's handsomely rugged face makes my stomach flutter wildly. "What are you doing?" He stalks closer, setting a mug on the nightstand.

Coffee.

"You've brought me coffee?"

"You're running a tad late," he says, his bodyguard demeanor sliding into place. That's when I allow my gaze to really look at him. Dressed in his uniform — a white button-up that seems to be stretched over tightly packed muscle, along with the dark slacks all my father's entourage wears — he looks ever the professional.

"How can I be late?"

"To meet with your little friend, Amber." He says her name with distaste all over his features. As if it tastes foul on his tongue.

I push up in bed, leaning my back on the headboard and lift the mug of steaming hot liquid to my mouth. "You don't like her?" I ask, after taking a tentative sip.

He scowls, which causes me to giggle. Dark eyes meet mine. "She's a bad influence," he mutters, settling on the small stool at my vanity. He looks strange sitting there. A big man on the tiny white chair.

"Everyone is an influence on others. It's up to you if you allow them to have that control over you."

He stares at me for a long while before nodding, then offering his response. "Seems like my little flower is pretty intelligent for a little girl."

"And I've told you before, I'm not—"

"I know, baby girl, I just enjoy watching that fire blaze in your eyes when I annoy you," he says. The side of his mouth kicks up into a full-blown smirk that has me shifting under the covers.

"Fuck you, Callan," I bite out, teasing him, taunting him, and he smirks.

"Say that again, baby girl," he threatens with a deep growl, animalistic and feral. And it's so damn sexy all I want is for him to devour me.

"Fuck. You. Callan." I know I'm provoking the beast, but I'm aching for him.

He moves swiftly, pulling me off the bed, bending me over the edge until he can tug at my panties. Once they're sitting at my thighs, he rains down six harsh swats on my ass until I'm a trembling mess.

My knees are still shaky when he pulls my panties up and straightens me. Then, with a gentle touch on my chin, lifting it slightly so I'm looking directly into his eyes, he tells me, "Now, the next time you're bratty, I'll do that in public."

"You're—"

"Insufferable? An arsehole? Save it, sweetheart," he murmurs, bringing his lips to mine. "I've heard it all before. You want this" — he gestures between us with his index finger — "then you'll have to get over the fact that I want to fuck you senseless anywhere and everywhere."

He brushes his lips over mine. It's a gentle yet commanding gesture. My ass is still stinging from my punishment, but it's a delicious kind of pain. The kind I crave.

Callan has a way of stealing my breath, gripping my heart as if he's just pulled it from my chest. His tongue darts into my mouth, licking at mine. We're in a duel for more. Aching and needy, I press my body against his hard one. My soft curves mold to him as if I'm a second skin.

When he pulls away, I'm staring up at him with nothing more than short, quick breaths. Gently, he swipes at my cheeks. "You're so pretty when you cry."

"You like seeing me cry?"

The corner of his mouth quirks into a grin, a smirk that makes his face light up with hunger. "I like seeing you lost in pleasure. And I like knowing that I'm the one who gave it to you."

"You act like you want to claim and own me," I counter, folding my arms in front of my chest to keep myself guarded, but it's an act. I know that because there's nowhere I can go, nothing I can do to stop my feelings for this man.

"All of you, even your pretty little pussy and ass too." He chuckles, earning him a swat from me.

"Do you have to be so vulgar?"

"Blossom, you love it when I'm vulgar. In fact." He leans in, his mouth latching onto my neck, his teeth biting down as he sucks the flesh into his mouth so hard it elicits a yelp from me. He pulls away, admiring his handiwork. "You love when I'm filthy because you're a dirty little girl." He steps back, releasing me from his hold.

"So, what do we do now?"

"Now you go shower, get dressed, and we need

to go shopping for a dress. The charity ball your father requested I escort you to is tomorrow," he says.

"Shit, I forgot about it. Do I have to go?"

"Yes. He won't be there, so he needs you to represent the Parker family," Callan offers.

"And you're my plus one?" I question incredulously.

He nods easily as if it's nothing. But it's not nothing. This is something. This is . . .

"It's work, Madison, not a date," he assures me as if he can see my mind working rapidly at the thought of dating him.

"I never said it was." My retort is met with a chuckle.

"You think I can't see how your pretty little head works, Blossom?" He leans closer as if he's about to impart some wisdom upon me. "I know what that filthy little mind of yours desires. I've been around far longer than you have, and I know exactly what a woman wants and needs."

"You're overly confident, Mr. O'Leary," I tell him. "I would suggest you don't assume what's going on in my head, because I'm not that transparent." I smile, placing my hands on his chest in an attempt to push him away.

He's a savage. And I want more. So much more. My phone hisses with a text message from the nightstand, breaking our contact, and I wonder if it's my dad or if it's my best friend. I'm about to pick it up when the chirpy ringtone I set as my father's sings to me.

"Hi, Daddy," I answer, settling myself on the edge of the bed.

Callan narrows his gaze, watching me intently, and I can see the inner workings of his mind. He's going to do something.

"Pumpkin, how are you?" He sounds genuinely concerned. It's not like him, but I let the smile on my lips stay because it feels good to have him actually worry about me.

"I'm fine, Dad," I respond as my bodyguard kneels on the floor at my feet. His big, rough hands push my knees apart, opening me to his stare.

I shake my head, but he just shrugs. Even though I attempt to press my legs closed, he's too strong, and I fail miserably.

"That's good. When I get back, we should go out to the lake house and spend some quality time together," he says, his tone even more pressing. Something urgent causes me to frown.

"That sounds good." My response drops when Callan leans in and trails the wet tip of his tongue over my sensitive inner thigh. He continues to copy the action on the other leg, and my body responds in kind.

"Listen, that charity ball tomorrow night. I need you to collect an award they'll be announcing, and I've just spoken to Hudson—"

"I'm not going with him," I whimper into the phone when my tormentor grazes my panty-clad clit with his teeth.

"What's happened?"

"He's an asshole, Dad," I retort hotly. Anger at the memory of what Hudson did races through me, mixed with desire from Callan's ministrations on my pussy swirling through me. My hand pushing at his head, but it's no use. The man is on a mission to make me come while I'm on the phone.

"Language, young lady!"

"Sorry, but he was here a few days ago, and . . . Well, and he hurt me."

"What?" The tone of my father's voice rises an octave as it drips with incredulousness. "Was O'Leary there? Did he sort him out?"

"Callan was here," I mumble as the man in question slips a finger into my hot core, pumping the digit in slow movements. In and out. "He . . . he . . . I mean, he helped," I manage to voice before another finger enters me.

"Good. I'll be talking to Hudson. He was always such a good boy," my father responds, sounding truly saddened by the change in my now ex-boyfriend.

My body arches as Callan lashes my wet lips with his tongue. "Can I call you tomorrow?" I ask, hoping my father will hang up.

"Yes, honey. I'll be in meetings most of the morning, but call me after lunch. I'm sorry I haven't been a better father," he tells me as my peak rises. I'm about to leap from the cliff when my father sighs once more. "I love you, pumpkin."

"I love you too," I respond, my tone clearly raspy.

"Always." He hangs up as Callan's fingers crook inside me, hitting that special spot that sees sparks flying from all around me. My toes curl into the mattress, and

I cry out his name, over and over again. I'm on my back, arching from the mattress as I claw at the bedspread, gripping it with white knuckles.

As I slowly come down from my euphoric high, I open my eyes to find the culprit of my orgasm smirking down at me.

"Like I said, Blossom, I have no morals. Perhaps next time, you can call *me* Daddy while I fuck that pretty little arse. Get dressed, we're leaving in twenty." With that, he rises and leaves me to finish my coffee and smile at his filthy mouth.

But I can't deny he's right. I want him. I want this more than I should, and I know it's only going to end in tears because he isn't going to work for my father forever, and soon, he'll want to go back to England.

That thought tightens an ache in my chest.

It's been over a month since I've last cut myself. Since Callan, I've not even had an inkling to do it. With him, I forget all the shit in my mind. I leave behind the darkness and look forward. My fingertips instinctively move to the scars. The various silver marks that line my otherwise smooth skin.

I'm not her anymore.

I close my eyes and pray, *I'm not her anymore.*

FIFTEEN

CALLAN

Tomorrow is the gala event, the charity fundraiser and I have to escort Madison. But as the day her father arrives back looms, I think about how this girl is going to be the worst addiction to kick. Most women I've been with are out the door before I even have time to learn their name, but with Madison, I want more. It's like she's embedded deep within me.

The kitchen is quiet when I settle on the chair and open my laptop. My coffee is steaming beside me as I open the emails I need to respond to. I lift the mug, sipping on the scalding liquid while I click on the browser and read through more research. I've been talking to Oliver about Madison's condition. When I saw the scars on her thighs and just below her belly button, I knew there was something deeply rooted.

She told me about her mother leaving, how she'd been bullied, and all that culminated in her resorting to hurting herself. Sadly, as a teenager, she kept her pain inside, whereas I went out to kill as many men as I could.

Oliver's response to my questions is long and drawn out. He's gone into the psychological side of it. About why she craves the pain, why she'd look to BDSM, spanking, whipping, perhaps even caning for her release. When someone holds onto their sadness, their pain so deep, there has to be some form of exit.

His advice is to teach her, take her and show her the pleasure that stems from a caning, rather than permanent damage. Which then leads him to believe she's a masochist — she needs the pain.

The memory of what she's done boils my blood. The thought of her hurting herself sends me into a rage, and all I see is red.

Last night, I watched her sleep. The gentle rise and fall of her chest was hypnotic. I spent an hour in the pool house staring at the ceiling, my body humming with the anticipation of being near her again, of being inside her again.

She's like a shot of whiskey, warm, intense, and she burns all the way down to my chest. And as much as I know I shouldn't, with each day that passes, I no longer give a fuck. I want to drink more of her, I want every fucking drop. Until she's in my veins, in my bloodstream.

"Good morning," her voice comes from the doorway. When I turn to look at her, I can't stifle the growl that leaves my lips. Dressed in a pair of white cotton shorts and a pale blue tank top, her long brown hair in messy waves only solidifies how beautiful she is.

Intoxicating.

"You're ready?" I ask. My voice is raspy, and she notices.

Quirking her eyebrow at me, she asks, "Almost. Just wanted to get something to eat. Is that okay?" Her words cause a soft smile to play on her glossy lips. Taking calculated steps toward me, she reaches for my tie, tugging it closer to her, and I find myself allowing her the control between us. For now.

"Of course, baby girl." My response is met with a

grin.

"Thank you, Mr. O'Leary," she quips. Leaning down until her face is next to mine, she plants a soft kiss on my scruffy cheek. Even though I haven't shaved, she keeps her lips on the stubble, almost as if she's enjoying the feel of it on her mouth.

"Blossom, if you keep that up, we'll be later than you already are. Your father booked an appointment with a boutique downtown, so you better get that pretty little mouth off me right now, or I'll fuck it until you're gagging."

She steps backward, her gaze piercing me. "You keep making these promises, and you never deliver." She giggles, turns, and busies herself making two slices of toast.

I watch her move around the space. Once she's eaten, she washes the plate and sets it on the drying rack.

"I'll wait outside," she tells me while I finish up my emails.

Moments later, I head out, finding her at the car in the long driveway. She's standing at the back door tapping on her phone, so she doesn't notice me coming

214

up behind her. Wrapping my arms around her waist, I pull her against me, causing a squeal to fall from her lips.

"Don't tease me, baby girl. It's rude," I whisper in her ear.

"You're always rude, so why can't I be?"

I plant a kiss on her cheek before answering. "Because I'm an arsehole, remember?"

"Oh yeah. Okay, Asshole, let's go." She giggles when I set her down and pull open the door for her. She slips into the seat, and I don't hide the fact that I stare at her long legs, her skin a soft shade of caramel that makes my cock ache. She's stunning. Silky smooth skin I want to taste every day. The thought of me actually wanting more than a month with her is jarring. I'm not the type of man who could give her a forever. Shaking my head to clear those thoughts, I slip into my seat and start the car.

She doesn't speak the whole ride from the house to the store. I'm thankful because it gives me time to think about how I'm going to ask my father to let me stay here. To be with her. We pull up outside a multitude of stores, where I notice Amber standing outside a boutique talking to a man who looks very much like the asshole I punched a few days ago. When he turns around, I note it is him.

"Why is your best friend with that arsehole?" I practically growl.

Madison scoots forward. Her eyes are wide as she watches Amber lean up on tip toes to kiss said dickhead on the mouth; but this is no friendly peck, this is a full-blown make-out session on the sidewalk. I start the engine, pull out onto the road, and drive down toward the lower end of the street.

"What are you doing?" Madison questions from behind me.

"We're going to another store," I bite out through clenched teeth.

She places a hand on my shoulder. The gentle touch burns through the material, causing me to jolt away from her. "I'm sorry." Her voice is timid, shy even, and I cast a quick glance at her as I pull into a parking lot.

"Don't you ever apologize to me, baby girl," I tell her with emotion thick and heavy in my tone. "You're perfect, and I hate to see that someone you trust is out there backstabbing you." My voice is urgent as I explain this to her. There's far too much affection in her gaze, and for the first time since I've been with her, I revel in it.

"I'm a big girl."

"I know, but you don't need that in your life," I inform her.

"I need you in my life," she retorts quickly, the words falling like leaves from a tree in autumn. The way her eyes glisten reminds me of happiness — warm, loving, and drenched with warmth. Looking at her makes me want to claim her for real, perhaps for longer than just the thirty days.

"Let's go. You need a dress." I turn away before I say something I'll regret later. *But will you regret it?* Pushing open the door, I shove the wayward thought out of my mind for now. *For now.* She follows me without needing me to open her car door, and I wonder if I've upset her. But then she reaches for me, her arm snakes itself through mine, and I can't stop the swell of pride in my chest.

This is new. So very new I'm astounded by how comfortable it is for her to hold onto me. For me to be the one she turns to when she wants safety. As we walk into the mall, I take in the shops and steer her toward a small boutique that seems like it might have what we're looking for.

The sales assistant offers a smile when we enter. "Good morning, how can I help?"

"My girlfriend would like a dress for an event we're attending tomorrow evening," I tell her and immediately notice Madison's reddened cheeks when my gaze lands on her.

"Perfect. Is there a particular color you had in mind?" the woman asks Madison who still seems in utter shock that I referred to her as my girlfriend. *Don't worry, darling, so am I,* I think to myself.

"Black, something classic and elegant," I respond for her, to which she nods slowly.

"Perfect, follow me." We get another megawatt smile, and I watch the sweet girl I'm slowly starting to care for walk toward rows of pinks, silvers, reds, and blacks. She reaches for one dress that's a soft peachy-orange, and I can't hear them talking, but Madison offers me a quick, naughty glance, then she heads into the changing room.

Passing the time, I stroll through the shop looking at various items I picture Madison wearing, but my mind drifts to tearing each piece of clothing from her frame and taking her in every which way known to man — and some not known.

"What do you think?" Her tentative voice comes from behind me. Spinning on my heel, I come face to face with the most beautiful woman I've ever seen in a dress that has every inch of my dick throbbing against my zipper.

The fabric looks like cotton candy, soft to the touch, as it hugs every curve of her hourglass frame. Her tits are pushed up, causing the scooping neckline to offer a glimpse of her cleavage. Her tits are beautiful, tempting, and I imagine tugging the neck of this dress down while I feast hungrily on her nipples.

It's not black, but it's perfect. A floor-length gown which hides the shoes she's wearing. When she twirls, though, that's when I can't stop my cock from hardening further. The back is lowcut, stopping just above her ass. The caramel skin of her back is smooth, shimmering in the low lights of the store from the body lotion I know she loves to use

Thin gold chains hold the back of her dress from left to right to stop the damn thing from falling from her shoulders. As she faces me again, I realize I haven't responded to her question, but I'm still shocked speechless. If I thought she was beautiful before, I was dead wrong. This woman is fucking stunning.

"Callan?" She says my name in question, snapping me from my daze.

"Blossom," I utter, closing the distance between us. "I hate this dress." My voice is a low growl in her ear, causing a shiver to travel over her body.

"What? Why?" She looks genuinely concerned at my words, her mouth pouting in the most seductive bow that makes me want to suck her lips into my mouth and bite down on them, reveling in her flavor.

"You look far too exquisite. Every man in his right mind will want you tomorrow night. I can't have that happening," I tell her honestly.

"Is that you admitting you like me?" she quips playfully. "Because, Mr. O'Leary, I like you too," Madison murmurs, and I'm tempted to take her back into that changing room and fucking her into submission.

"That's me admitting the thoughts that are running through my mind right now are far from clean, Blossom," I murmur in her ear. Turning her to face the mirror, I position myself behind her, showing her how we look together. The stark contrast between the hue of her dress against the black and white of my clothes is harsh, but it looks incredible.

"We scrub up pretty well," she tells our reflection.

"You look stunning," announces the sales assistant as she appears. "Is this the one?" she questions, and Madison glances at me in the mirror. I nod in agreement.

"Yes, we'll take this one," my girl responds. *My girl*. Jesus, I'm turning soft.

Madison disappears into the changing room to take the dress off while I pay for the item. The woman stares at me for a moment before sliding the plastic card through the machine. I've signed and gotten a receipt by the time my girl comes out.

"You paid?" she gasps as she hands the dress to be wrapped up.

"Of course." I smile, wrapping an arm around her waist, pulling her into me as I revel in how well she fits there. After everything I've done in my life, all the good, all the bad, nothing can compare to having her nestle her head in the crook of my arm.

On our way back to the car, I go to open the back door, but Madison's hand stalls my movement. "I want to sit up front with you," she informs me with a smile.

Offering a nod, I pull open the passenger door and help her into the seat. Once I've placed the package with her dress in the backseat, I slip in beside her.

"I like being up here," she says. A soft laugh tumbles freely from her, and those eyes — god, those honey-colored eyes shimmer with excitement and happiness.

"You sure you want to sit here? You never know who could see us."

She shakes her head. "Yes, now that I'm your girlfriend" — she leans in, planting a chaste kiss on my cheek — "I guess I can sit here every day."

Chuckling, I start the car and turn toward home. "Don't get cheeky, baby girl. I only said that because the woman in the store probably thought I was your dad."

"Ha, you're such a liar. You like me."

I don't look at her when I respond. "Maybe. I think you're sexy, beautiful, and completely and utterly fuckable."

"Well, I think you're hot, grumpy, and old, so there's that too."

"Old enough to spank your ass for disrespecting me," I counter, dragging my gaze over to her for a second before focusing back on the road.

"I think you'd just like to spank me because it would turn you on."

Her feisty mouth makes me want to pull into a parking lot and show her just how much she turns me on, but I don't. She sits back, satisfied she's won *this* round, but she doesn't know I'm planning to make her pay for her sassy comments.

There's a surefire way to make her squirm, and I'm dying to do it at the event. While we're amongst the elite of Chicago, I'm going to make sure she never forgets who's in charge.

"You know, Blossom, I have to grab something for

tomorrow. I want you to lock yourself in the house. I'll only be thirty minutes," I tell her.

She glances my way, and from the corner of my eye, I can tell she's trying to assess just what I'm planning, but she won't.

"I'll be fine. I doubt he'll come around here again, and anyway, I'm sure Lawrence will be around." Her voice is nonchalant, but the thought of any other man being close to her has me gripping the steering wheel in a white-knuckle grip.

"Who?" I glance her way as I pull into the driveway of the mansion.

"My father's security guard who stays on the property."

"Mmm." I sound jealous. I hear it in the tone of my huff.

She smiles as I cut the engine and glance at her once more. "You're cute when you're jealous," she remarks. She shoves the door open, huffing as she exists the vehicle, but before she can get away, I'm rounding the front of the car. I easily grip her arm and pull her closer to me.

224

I grasp her chin between my thumb and index finger, then lean in, inhaling her sweet-scented perfume. "Let's get one thing straight, baby girl," I growl, lowering my mouth to hers, brushing my lips against hers slightly, which makes her lean closer, needing connection, but I don't offer it. "I'm not cute. I've never been cute, so next time you want to piss me off, call me cute."

"What would you do if I did call you . . . you know." She waves her hand in the air, not uttering the damn word.

"I'd punish you."

Her breathing hitches. Her pulse riots in her neck, thumping against that spot I want to taste, lick, and nibble on. "And if I want to be punished?" She breathes the words, and my cock responds with a *fuck yes*.

"You wouldn't like my punishments, sweetheart, because when — and yes, I said when — I do punish you, it will not be pleasurable. I'll make sure your pretty honey-colored eyes sparkle like golden raindrops. And I'll make sure you curse me until I reward you again."

Her tongue flicks out, trailing along her lips, making them shimmery and wet. "There's nothing you can do to me that will scare me off. So, if that's what you're doing here." She sighs. "It won't work."

The air is heavy with desire. I know she's nervous. Her eyes are like windows into her heart, her soul, and deep down, she may act like this strong, sassy little minx, but I know she's scared of this.

I'm happy she's scared. Because I know what kind of man I am. Selfish, rude, and I'll break her. Not physically, but emotionally. I know I'll shatter her heart when it's time to say goodbye. As good as this feels, having her in my arms, I wonder if it's a passing faze for her.

And soon, I'll no longer be employed by her father. Which means that somewhere along the line, I may have to walk away.

But it doesn't stop me wanting her.

SIXTEEN

MADISON

Spinning on my heel, I leave him standing there as I head into the house. I don't look back to see if he's following me, but when I hear the crunch of shoes on the paved cobblestones echo toward me from the open doorway, I know he has. Making my way straight for the kitchen, I grab a bottle of chilled water from the fridge, and that's when he finally joins me.

As much as I want this, I feel a heaviness in the pit of my stomach. Callan's not a man who'll stick around. There's something in his eyes, in the way he acts that shows he remains aloof. Even though I'm right there in the room with him, there's a part of the man hidden behind high concrete walls. And that part reminds me he can easily hurt me. But each time I'm around him, I feel more.

He stares at me for a moment too long, his gaze flickering between my lips and my eyes. It's heated. Burning me from the inside out. He's like a goddamn match against my blood, which has turned to gasoline, and I know he can see it. It's as if he enjoys watching me burn for him.

"Do you really get off acting like an asshole?" My voice comes out breathy, and I can't stop admonishing myself for acting like this around him. He makes me crazy; he turns me into a teenage girl again, and I don't like it. I'm stronger than that, but as his knuckles trace the curve of my cheek, dropping to the slope of my neck, I tremble.

"I do, but more than that, it gets you off, too. I see it in your pretty eyes, Madison. If you didn't want this," he says, gripping the nape of my neck. "If you didn't want me," he confirms, stepping closer, our bodies aligned perfectly with his rigidness pressing against my stomach. "Then you wouldn't still be standing here waiting for me to kiss you."

"I'm not waiting for anything, Callan," I inform

him, lifting my chin slightly, which only brings my mouth closer to his. Inches separate us. The proximity of his body to mine causes desire to tighten low in my belly. My core quivers, and I'm needy once more.

"Then you best go and get that dress hung up properly for tomorrow."

"You don't have to come with me." I finally pull away from him, needing space from the overbearing man who seems to have such power over me it leaves me both speechless and motionless.

My knees are wobbly when I finally walk toward the exit of the kitchen, leaving Callan at the counter. "I'll be right beside you all night, Blossom. And when you're ready to come home, I'll be the one to bring you here safely." He voices his promise in a deep, rumbling lilt.

"Then I suppose it's settled." I smile, stalking out of the kitchen. I know he's heading out, so when I reach my bedroom, I drop my purse on the vanity counter and stroll over to the balcony window to watch the SUV pulling out of the drive. I wonder where he's going.

Callan has been gone all morning. Last night when he arrived back from Sins, he went straight for the pool house. I've spent the day in my room reading, trying not to think about what's happening between us. Also, trying to push the thought of the event tonight from my mind.

My purse vibrates wildly on the wooden top, and I know exactly who it is. My best friend — at least, the person I used to call my best friend — must be calling to find out where I was yesterday. As soon as the vibration stops, it starts again. Sighing, I pull it from my purse to find Amber's name flashing at me.

I don't want to talk to her. I don't need to hear the excuses and lies, but I swipe my finger over the screen and place the device to my ear.

"Madi?" her voice is shrill over the speaker, causing me to wince.

"Hey."

"Where were you? I waited for ages. Are you okay?" Her concern is fake, her voice heavy with sugary-sweet lies, and anger bubbles through me. Her friendship has been like a poison slowly trickling through my life, and I didn't know it until I saw her with my ex-boyfriend in the middle of the sidewalk. I had been blind. Wanting so much to be accepted into the life my father forced me into.

The limelight.

The fame that comes along with being a senator's daughter.

I hate it.

"I decided to wear something from my closet," I tell her easily. The lie slipping from my lips and hanging in the air.

"You can't be serious?" she questions incredulously, unbelieving that I'm going to wear something *last season* or even perhaps a hand-me-down from my mother, but there's no way I can even do that. She walked out when I was a child and never looked back. When she died, my father had everything she'd ever had in the house donated to charity.

"I am. In fact, I'm thinking of perhaps a plain black dress. Simple and elegant."

She gasps loudly, and I can only picture the shock

and horror on her face.

"I'll see you later, Amber." I hang up before she has time to respond or retort.

There's been this long-standing joke that black is boring or old school, but I don't need to impress anyone. Not anymore. That's a lie. There is only one person I want to impress, and that's Callan.

I never had a plan when I first walked up to him in the parking lot of Sins. I didn't even have a clue what he'd say to me, or what his reaction would be when I asked him for a ride on his motorcycle. But when his gaze dropped to mine, I knew he would be trouble.

I'm convinced a man like that can never love someone. Hell, I don't even know if I can love him. But I can enjoy the time he's here. Even if we only have a few days left. And who knows? My father might return earlier, and I'll once again have a new driver or bodyguard. Maybe Daddy will finally retire. Although, I doubt that. He enjoys the limelight far too much.

Toeing off my shoes, I sigh with relief that my feet are finally on the soft, plush carpeting. I need to get ready, but my mind is still spinning from the whiplash of Callan O'Leary, and as I reach my bathroom and turn on the shower, I glance in the mirror at the girl that's smitten. I can see it in my eyes. There's a soft, pink glow in my cheeks. My eyes are glazed with want.

The spray is warm, but it does nothing to calm me. Tonight, I'll see Hudson again. I'll also come face to face with Amber, and even though I don't want to cause a scene, I have a feeling there will be one. My best friend is not someone who will take something lying down. I don't care if she wants my ex-boyfriend, but for her to lie to me, to tell me she's my friend when all along she's probably been fucking him behind my back, it makes me more angry than sad.

Serves me right for dating the *good boy* as my father puts it. Hudson is everything my dad would want in a son-in-law. He's the type of guy who would fit into our lifestyle without fuss. All the dinner parties, the clothes, and etiquette. It's sad you're bombarded with so many rules and regulations but still turn out to be an asshole.

I'm stepping out of the shower when I hear shuffling in my bedroom. The gentle echo of shoes on my carpet makes my heart leap to my throat. It can't be

Hudson. He wouldn't come back here, not after what happened.

Wrapping a towel around my body, I head into the room to find it empty, but on the bed is a small silver box. The square shape offers no hint as to what it could be as it shimmers from where I'm standing. A bright orange bow glints in the dim light of my nightstand lamp.

When I reach the bed, I run my finger along the silvery edge. My mind flitting between what it is and just how Callan found something that he's now placed on my bed.

"I hope you'll wear it tonight," a deep voice comes from my doorway, startling me.

Spinning around, I find him leaning against my doorframe dressed in a dark pair of slacks that hug his impossibly muscled thighs. The white shirt he's wearing looks like it's just been pressed, no creases whatsoever, and a tie hangs loose around his neck. The top four buttons of his shirt are undone, and the smooth skin that peeks at me is a tease of what's beneath the crisp material.

"You're buying me gifts?" I quip, untying the

ribbon and flicking open the lid of the box. Inside, on black velvet, is a silver plug. The jewel on the end, a deep burnt orange, is the color of a darkening sunset. "A butt plug?"

"It is." This time he smirks, the corner of his mouth lifting slightly, his full lips taunting me with only that sinful grin.

"I'd love to wear it," I tell him, noting his dark brows shoot up in surprise. "Would you like to insert it for me?" Tentatively, I lift it from the cushioning and glance up at Callan, whose eyes are as dark as night.

"Drop your towel, Blossom, and bend over so that pretty little ass is open for me," he orders gruffly. His voice laced with desire, with need and want. Slowly, I allow the fluffy material to pool at my feet, then turn and lower myself to the bed. My backside pointed toward him, my legs spread a few inches, giving him access to me.

"Like this?" I murmur into the mattress as his hand cups the globe of my ass.

"You're a naughty fucking tease, baby girl," he grunts, and I know he's affected by me, my body, and

I realize that even though he might not stick around forever, I can learn, grow under his watchful eye.

He moves behind me. A snap of a plastic cap alerts me he had planned this all along. He had lube ready and waiting; he baited me, and I fell for it. Hook. Line. Sinker. I'm his, and there's no more denying it.

He works gently, his fingers teasing my tight entrance, then I feel the cold metal pressing at my hole. Torturously, he inches the metal plug into my ass. I've only ever done this once before. It was Hudson and I experimenting, but he hated everything about it. Now I realize he just didn't want *me*. Callan though, something about his possessiveness confirms there's so much more between us, and I wonder if he'll ever commit to it.

When the plug slips into me, fully seated, he gently massages the cheeks of my ass. "Such a pretty girl," he coos, pressing a kiss to my lower back where my spine meets my rear. "Stand." His order is a whisper along my skin, and I rise without question. The fullness of my body causes me to wobble, but Callan's strong arms are around me instantaneously.

"This is . . ." I'm not sure what to say, allowing my

words to filter into nothing.

"Tell me," he commands in a serious yet dominating tone.

I meet those eyes that shimmer with desire. As many times as Callan has looked at me, there's not been affection in his stare. Merely need. Nothing that could ever allow me to mistake him for caring, for him feeling anything more than what this really is.

"I feel full," I tell him finally.

He nods, pulling my naked body against his. I mold to him. All my soft curves fit into his hard edges, and I try to steel myself from feeling anything more than basal desire.

"It's different."

"Tonight, I'll show you different, Blossom," he vows. "There's nothing more I want right now than to bend you over and show you just how hard you make me, but I promised your father I'd escort you safely to the event, shadow you for the evening, and then return you to your pretty princess bed."

Those last few words are said with derision. He doesn't believe I'm the innocent girl I'm meant to portray.

Fuck, neither do I, to be honest.

"And then what?" I quip, tipping my chin up to face him head on. Our gazes locked in a stand-off. I can't look away. He doesn't. The heat between us is at boiling point when he finally steps away from me.

"Then I'll fuck you until you can't walk. Tomorrow you'll spend in bed, recovering from the agony my cock will put you in."

I should be appalled. Any woman would be angry at his filthy words, but I'm far from it. In fact, I'm so turned on I squirm under his heated gaze.

"You really do have a high regard of yourself and your abilities, Mr. O'Leary."

He chuckles, the corner of his eyes crinkling ever so slightly, but instead of aging him, it only makes him look younger.

"You do underestimate me, Ms. Parker." He leans in, his lips whispering over the smooth skin of my neck. I shudder when the heat of his warm breath hits me. "Because, I assure you, I wear my confidence proudly, and the only reason I do is because I know the moment your pretty caramel thighs are either side of my head, and my tongue is dipping deep into that sweet, tight hole, you'll forget your own fucking name. And you will do, because the only thing you'll remember is *my* name, Callan O'Leary."

SEVENTEEN

CALLAN

I turn and leave her in the bedroom, no doubt still blushing from my illicit promise. The thought of tasting her, of bending her over and licking my way from her clit to that tight ass, draws a groan from my chest.

And as much as I'd love to skip the party, it's imperative we attend. There are a few people who'll be there who need to see her. She also needs to collect her father's award for some or other title he doesn't deserve.

Pulling my phone from my pocket, I tap out a message to Oliver. He must already be there because his response is a mere "Okay". In the foyer, I shrug on my jacket, fasten my tie, and by the time the knot is choking me, Madison graces me with her presence. The dress I recall from yesterday is stunning, her curves are deliciously taunting, and I have to fight against the hard-on in my slacks.

"I'm ready." She smiles up at me.

"Are you wearing panties?" I question, taking in her appearance hungrily.

She nods. "Yes. A thong, actually, and it's lace." Her words are feathered along the collar of my shirt. The effect is my dick throbbing against my zipper.

"Let's go," I tell her gruffly, jerking the door open and allowing her to exit first. She sways her hips marginally as she walks toward the car. The little tease will pay for that later. She'll pay for everything with those beautiful holes of hers. I'm going to devour every inch of her, and when I'm done, she will be sated.

Not waiting for me to open the door, she pulls it open and slips into the passenger seat. I don't know how it will look with her sitting up front, but tonight, I don't give a fuck. She's mine for the evening, and I'm going to make the most of it. Knowing I can't have any normal relationship with her, I have to appease my hunger by stolen moments like a fucking teenager.

Once I'm in the driver's seat and the engine is

rumbling, I steer us down the driveway, through the black metal gates, and down to the Palmer House Hotel where the party is being held this evening.

The scent of Madison hangs heavily in the air, the gentle citrus of her orange blossom perfume the only thing I can smell. She makes me want more, every goddamn inch of her. Soon I'll be gone, and she'll be moving on to better things, but I'll never forget her fragrance. The way she challenges every ounce of restraint I own. Somehow, even after just the time we've spent together since her father hired me, I'm addicted to her, and my concrete plan to tear down the Parker name is gone.

The past six months since I arrived in the city, I've watched her. She's been my special project, following her to see where she went, what she enjoyed, and now, I'm in deep. It's stupid, I shouldn't have done it, but something about her called to me.

"You're quiet," she offers, leaning against the chair, her head tilted toward me as she regards me. I feel her gaze on me, burning through my walls, piercing past those barriers I put up a long time ago.

"I'm thinking."

"About?" she asks, turning her body so she's facing me. Once again, my skin flames as she scorches me with those dark eyes. I don't look at her, instead focusing my gaze on the road ahead.

I can see the hotel in the distance, and I pray to a God that long ago abandoned me and my family, hoping I can hold onto the darkness lurking just beneath the surface. I want to unleash it on her just to hear her screaming my name. Just to watch her body writhe as I fuck her hard, mercilessly, until she's spent.

"You know, Callan, you may hide behind that mask, but I see you," she confesses what I already know. Something about this woman has stirred something within me, something long lost, and no matter how much I try, I'll never be able to shake it.

"We're here," I respond, ignoring her earlier words, hoping she'll drop it. *I don't want her to see me*, I lie to myself. Pushing open the door, I drop the keys into the hand of the valet and round the front to help Madison from the vehicle. She slips her small, delicate hand in mine, and once again, a jolt shoots through me and my veins are alight. As if a match has been dropped on me and I'm burning for her.

Jesus, O'Leary, get a hold of yourself.

I escort the woman beside me into a large ballroom, which is opulent, decked out in crystal chandeliers, plush Merlot-colored carpets, and shimmering iron trim along the walls holding the wallpaper in place.

Picture frames hang along the walls, looking like they belong in a historic building like Windsor Castle rather than a rich man's playground in the middle of Chicago. Everything looks like it's been dipped in liquid gold and hung up for people who have far too much money to bask in. And bask they do.

My gaze roams over the crowd as people walk up to Madison to greet her. She's long since let go of my hand, but I still feel her. She's close, so much so I can still smell her citrus and floral perfume.

"And this is Callan O'Leary." Her voice steals my attention, and I'm brought back to the present.

The man glances at me with a confident smirk, and I almost allow my dislike of him to show, but I manage to school it just as Madison glances at me with a smile. There's something about him I don't like.

"He works for my father, watching over me like a hawk." Her innocent words cause him to lift those dark inquisitive brows.

"Mr. O'Leary." His voice cuts through me like a hot knife through ice. The man is the spitting image of her asshole ex-boyfriend, Hudson. "It's lovely to make your acquaintance." His mouth lifts into a satisfied smirk because he knows I'm the one who fucked-up his son. The one thing he's not counting on is that I'd do it again.

When his son saunters over, his satisfied smirk has me twitching to wipe it off with a few liters of acid. Perhaps even dropping him in a bath of the shit. The man I would like to see six feet under is standing before me with a woman on his arm. Draped over him like an expensive piece of jewelry.

It's only when she snarks at Madison do I recognize the made-up Barbie doll. "You're really wearing that?"

"She is," I respond for my woman. "And I'm dying to drive her back home right now and show her just how beautiful I think she looks." I offer my hand to Hudson's father, whose name I missed. "It's good to meet you."

We shake before he grins. "Gregory Brockovich. I think you may have met my son, Hudson," he tells me, and it slowly sinks in with his words. Accusation. Clearly Hudson can't defend himself, so he ran to Daddy to help him.

"Yes, we've been lucky enough to make an acquaintance," I respond easily. Slipping my arm around Madison's waist, I offer the asshole a smirk before greeting. "We're off to mingle. We'll probably see you later."

With that, I lead my girl away from the tense conversation. All my life, I've dealt with war between families, and I don't want her to experience the shit that comes along with it. I saw it in Gregory's eyes. It dances like a flame. There was venom dripping from his smirk, giving away his feelings toward me about the fact that Madison is on my arm and not his precious boy's.

"Are you okay?" Madison looks up at me when we stop at the bar. There's a crease in her brow as she regards me. In this light, she looks so beautiful and innocent all I want to do is muss her up. Make sure when we walk back out of a dark corner, everyone will know

I've claimed her.

"I'm fine. I just realized the people in this room are just as bad as the ones we deal with back home." We're all sinners here. All out for ourselves, to ensure everyone knows our names. I think back to my own past and how the O'Learys along with the Morans have always been at odds.

It's easy to aim a gun, to pull the trigger, and it's easy to watch someone's life flash in their eyes before the light is snuffed out. I could easily do that right here, while looking into Hudson's shrewd glare. And I'd do it with a smile on my face.

That kind of training never leaves. It's always there, beneath the surface. The need to feel your enemies blood drip between your fingers. The cock of a fully loaded gun. The sharp hiss of the bullet leaving the barrel, and the sweet crimson spraying from the wound as it steals the lives of men like Seamus Moran, our lifetime enemy. They don't deserve to live.

"I knew a man like him," I answer finally. "They always saw their demise, but I couldn't very well go doing something stupid in the middle of a party." My response is accompanied with a sardonic grin, causing her brown eyes to blaze.

"I know you've killed people, but hearing you say it is strange." Her whisper is only for me to hear, and I love how close she is to me when she does lean in.

"Do I scare you?"

This time she lifts her gaze to mine. There's a gentleness that she regards me with. It's not pity, but concern. "You don't scare me at all, but you do worry me."

"Why? Life happens to everyone, but so does death. I used to just deliver it earlier than they were expecting." My words cause Madison to grip my arm, squeezing as if she really does worry about me. I've always scared everyone away, but with her, I can't find it in myself to do it anymore.

Her touch is what calms me. It's she who makes me realize I can do anything and she'd forgive me. But when my eyes land on our enemy, he smirks as if he knows something I don't. What he doesn't know is I never back down. I never let the other person win, because I'm good at what I do. And when I set my mind to it, nobody comes out alive.

We'll all bear scars of this war.

We'll all fight, but only one side can lose, and I'll ensure he pays for hurting her. If Hudson comes near Madison, he'll not see the light of day again.

"Madison, let's get drinks." I tug her close to me, which is my first mistake. The second is the way she curves her body into my hold. He sees it. He knows there's something about her. She's special to me, and as I turn toward the bar, I berate myself. I shouldn't have done it, but I couldn't let him think she's only here because I'm a guard. She's here for me.

I fucked up.

Big time.

"What was that?" She doesn't miss a fucking beat, questioning me as soon as we're out of earshot. "Callan—"

"Nothing to worry your pretty little head about, Blossom," I bite out, knocking on the oak counter of the bar to catch the attention of anyone who can pour me a fucking drink.

"Don't shut me out," she pleads, but I ignore her.

She's fucked with my head, and I just messed up. I've put her in danger, and she doesn't even realize how fucked up this could get. If she only knew I wouldn't think twice about taking Hudson and slicing him from head to toe just to watch him bleed all over the carpet of this ballroom just to get back at him for hurting her.

Three months ago, Carrick, my baby brother, flinched when we went to take out a lifetime enemy of our family. He couldn't do it, so I took the shot. I killed Seamus Moran because he took the life of Rick's fiancée. An eye for an eye. It's how we've always lived out life.

And now Hudson knows Madison means something to me. Something in his eyes tells me he wouldn't stop at hurting her just to get back at me.

I should never have fucked her. Never have touched or kissed her. Carrick warned me, and I didn't fucking listen. The barman sets down a tumbler with a double shot of amber liquid, which I swallow down without asking what it is.

"Another. Better yet, bring the bottle," I order, and he nods. I watch as he moves around the bar, pulling the bottle of Macallan from the shelf and setting it beside my glass. This is what I need. This is always what calms the storm raging within me. War wages, but as I gulp down the alcohol, I know I'll ease the tension that knots my muscles.

"Callan." Madison pleads my name, causing me to finally look at her.

"Tonight, you'll go home with one of your father's men. I'll be staying at my brother's place. There's shit I need to sort out."

"What?" Her dark eyes widen in shock at my harsh words, which are spit in frustration. It's not her fault. I'm the asshole who put her in danger, but I need to take my anger out on someone. Anyone. And she's right here.

"You're such an—"

"Arsehole?" I finish her sentence. "Tell me something I don't know by now, baby girl." I gulp down another shot and a third before she finally pulls my arm until I'm looking at her again. "But I need to sort something out, okay?"

"Are you really going to send me home alone?" she questions, picking up her white wine. The Chardonnay glistens in the glass as she lifts it to her mouth. Plump, shimmery lips purse as she sips the liquid.

"Listen to me, Blossom." I pull her closer, my hand on her hip, my fingers digging into her soft curves. "My job is to keep you safe. I need you to listen to me and stop fighting me at every turn. For once, just let me do what I was hired to do, and that's ensure you're safe. Stop being a brat about this."

She tugs her arm from my grip, hissing in my ear, "Fuck you, Callan O'Leary. Fuck you and your so-called dangerous life. If I wanted a safe life, I would've stayed with Hudson. Perhaps he'll make me come with this plug in my tight little ass." Her words are for me, savage and brutal, cold and calculating, but they drip with poisonous desire.

And I know she feels something more for me.

And I know deep down, the more I push this woman away, the more she'll fight me tooth and nail until I'm the one kneeling at her feet.

EIGHTEEN

MADISON

He's not telling me something. I see the secrets he's hiding, and it makes me want to know more. I want to scoop out everything in his mind and devour it. Yes, I may be young, I may be more innocent than he's used to, but I'm not stupid.

"I didn't ask for love, Callan. I didn't ask for a fucking ring. I'm asking for you to actually let someone in for once in your goddamn life, but clearly, you can't," I bite out. Gulping down the wine, I slam the glass on the counter and stalk away from him.

His voice is rigid behind me, calling to me to stop, but I don't. I can't, because the fucking butt plug is making each step more difficult than the last. It feels good, I feel full, but I also feel needy. I want him to touch me, to stroke the ache hanging heavily on my core and ease it somewhat.

The hallway is dimly lit. There aren't many people around, and I easily push through the doorway of the stairwell. My back flush against the cool concrete as I inhale deeply, attempting to calm myself from the frustration Callan leaves in his wake.

He's like a storm, wreaking havoc on everything he touches, but as much destruction as he causes, he also offers me some kind of calm.

"Madison fucking Parker, if you don't—" He comes storming through the door to find me on the step, my arms curled around my legs, my ass at an angle on the concrete because it's uncomfortable to sit down. But he stalls as if he's in shock seeing me in this state. My eyes burn from unshed tears, but they're not from sadness. Rather from the frustration of wanting, needing, and craving a man who pushes me away at every turn.

I don't blink.

I don't allow them to fall.

Instead, I pin him with a glare. "Leave me alone, Callan," I retort, anger entwined in every word, lacing itself around me as I watch him breathe.

"Do you know how much danger you're in?" he growls. He fucking grunts like an animal about to devour its prey, and I know I'm the deer caught by the lion.

"What? Because you decided to piss off Hudson and his dad?" My words cause him to stall. He stops his approach and glares at me.

"I know men like him. He'll hurt you, kill you." Those words are not new to me. I've heard it all before. But I'm done playing kids games. I'm over being the frail flower everyone thinks I am.

"Why don't you check yourself, Callan?" I bite out, rising to full height. The sadness he caused is gone, and in its wake is something new. A strength I didn't know existed inside me. "I've been threatened before. Fuck, I've even been kidnapped before, so don't think for one second I'm some delicate flower you need to protect." I take a step closer to him, lowering myself from the stair until we're toe to toe. "Let me tell you something, Mr. O'Leary, I can fight a man off me. I can hold a gun, and I wouldn't flinch if I had to pull the trigger. So don't for one fucking minute think I need you to protect me."

My words cause another flare of anger, frustration, and something else I never knew existed inside him — respect. I'm certain I've convinced him. I'm sure after my show of strength he'll finally give me what I want.

But it all comes crashing down when he shakes his head.

"This time, you'll obey me." He grips my arm, tugging me out the door and toward the exit. We make our way hastily as my father's name is called, but there's nobody there to accept the award. The car is brought around only moments after we've stepped out into the chilly night, and I'm plonked into the passenger seat without a word. He locks me inside as he rounds the front, and then he's beside me. I have no choice but to allow him to take me home.

The silence that hangs between us in the space of the vehicle is stifling as he grips the steering wheel with a white-knuckle hold. The tension radiating off him holds my attention, it steals every inhale and exhale as I watch him command the vehicle through the streets.

I don't look at the road, my gaze focused on Callan. On his broad frame, his taut muscles beneath a beautiful suit. *We didn't even get to dance tonight.* The thought unbidden but saddening as it pops into my mind.

It's only moments later that we're pulling into the long driveway of the Parker mansion. He still hasn't spoken. He moves with precision, opening my door, helping me from the SUV. We make our way toward the house, and I watch him unlock it, shoving open the door and allowing me to step inside first. There are soft yellow lights all around the foyer, and when I look at Callan, he's cast in a gentle glow.

A devil inside an angel's body.

"You should get some sleep. I'll contact your father and inform him we missed the ceremony due to safety precautions. Then—"

"Callan—"

"I'm leaving now, Madison. Have a lovely evening."

He doesn't wait for me to say anything more, shutting the heavy wooden door behind him. I try to pull on it, but he's locked it.

He's left.

He walked out, and it's because of me.

It's been two days.

Long, dreary, and annoying days.

I woke up the night after the event to an empty bed. I had to remove the fucking plug from my ass in the shower. I ached. My whole body was alight with need, and there was nobody around to ease it. But that's not why I'm angry. That morning, I was informed Callan had given over the post as my bodyguard to someone else. Another man on my father's team to escort me around.

I don't mind so much. He's older, married, and he's only here for his paycheck, but it's the fact that Callan told me he was only going to sort something out stings. My chest aches because as much as I didn't admit it, I fell for him.

Sighing, I stare at the ceiling, wondering what he's doing, where he is. All my calls have gone unanswered. Even the messages I've sent him, both angry, forgiving, and wanting. He's not responded to any of them. I let my frustration out in a long text message. I told him everything that was on my mind, but even when I was brutally honest, he couldn't give me the same in return.

Perhaps it's better that he's gone. But as soon as I think that, my heart aches, my chest tightens with pain so acute it steals my breath. My emotions get the better of me when I remember how he felt, his touch, his filthy words, and the way he fit inside me like he was meant to be there.

A knock at my door startles me, and I'm on my feet in seconds. When I pull it open, I find my father standing on the other side. He looks stressed out, disheveled.

"Dad."

"Madison." He offers a curt nod and enters my room. He doesn't look at me, rather heads toward the window and stares out of it for a long while. "You were meant to be the good girl, looking after the Parker name," he starts, and I know what's coming.

"Look, Dad—"

He spins on his heel, glaring at me angrily. I've seen my father upset before, but the rage that seems to simmer from him is something else. "I trusted you, Madison. You asked to be treated like an adult, and I did. I left here for a month and have been called back a week early because you decided to galivant with your bodyguard."

"I did not *galivant*!" I retort hotly. "I fell in love!"

"Love? You're a child. You have no idea what love is. Hudson gave you—"

"Hudson?" I'm screeching, but I don't care. I hope the whole goddamn city hears me. "Did Hudson tell you how he came into my room to force me on the bed? Did Hudson tell you that he got beaten up by Callan because he hurt me?"

My father's mouth falls open in shock, and I take that as my cue.

"I didn't think so. Because you know what Hudson is? A fucking animal! At least Callan treated me like a lady. He respected me, made me smile."

"This is ridiculous. I've spoken to Mr. Brockovich. We're setting up your nuptials to Hudson. They're to take place in a week."

Rage shudders through me violently.

"What?" The word is hissed from my lips as I glare at my father, ready to set him alight with a mere glance.

"You heard me." There's tension wafting from him like a cheap cologne. He's always been relaxed, calm, but he seems on edge, which only makes me wary as to where he's been and why he's trying to once again ruin my life.

"You can't do this."

"I did," he says, stalking by me to my bedroom door. His fingers rake through his messy hair. There are dark circles under his eyes, and when he glances at me, he offers a look that tells me not to argue.

"Why, Dad?" It's me who crumbles to the floor, and for the first time in my life I show my father who I am. A scared little girl who needs her father to tell her it's going to be okay.

"I want you to pack a suitcase, something small. I've got two of my men ready to drive you out of the city," he says, the tone of his voice guarded, which only has the hair on the back of my neck raised with suspicion.

"What? Now?" I ask him, but he merely nods. His mind isn't here. It's so far away that when he looks at me again a second later I don't recognize the man standing in my bedroom.

"I'd like you to go to the lake house to think about your wedding plans," he says in an attempt to calm my racing heart, but it does nothing of the sort.

"This is ridiculous, Dad. Tell me what is going on? You can't hide things from me. I'm a grown woman, and I deserve to know why you're sending me away. If it's Hudson forcing you to do this, you can just fire him."

"You make it sound so terrible," he grunts. "I thought perhaps you could use the time away, Madison." He turns to me, but his eyes betray his words. I see the fear dancing in them. Something's very wrong. "And Hudson is a good boy."

"I'm not leaving until you tell me what's going on," I tell my father. But before he can respond, his phone chimes in the pocket of his jacket. His suit is wrinkled, telling me he's been awake all night, because if there's one thing about Magnus Parker, his suits are always pressed to perfection.

"Hello." His voice lowers, and he leaves my bedroom, stalking down the hallway to his office. I'm unsure what's going on, but this time, Callan must answer me. I pick up my phone and tap out a message, telling him my father wants to send me off to the damn lake house, marry Hudson, and I have no idea why.

I sit in silence, willing the phone to ring, to buzz. Anything. But as always, it doesn't. The black screen glares at me, taunting me. He's left, and he doesn't want me. It's clear when he told me this isn't forever, he meant it. Almost a month of knowing him, and I'm smitten like a damn teenager.

The men in my life are only making me crazy. Dad acting strange, Callan going MIA, nothing makes sense. And I have a feeling it's got to do with Gregory Brockovich. I recall the thug who wanted a folder from my father's office. He never came back for it, never contacted me again.

Which begs the question . . . Is he threatening my father directly?

NINETEEN

CALLAN

My blood simmers when I read her message.

There's nothing stopping me from going to her now and kidnapping her sweet little ass. But I know I can't. My mind has played out all the scenarios that this would work. How I'd be able to get Madison away from Hudson. The asshole doesn't deserve her.

When I reach the club and pull into the parking space beside Rick's SUV, I still feel the frustration coursing through me from walking out on her. The words she sent are like a fucking taunt. Back and forth, ping-ponging in my mind as I picture her with him. And with every thought, more rage warms my blood.

Thankfully, as I make my way to the apartment, I know I'll be alone. Rick's not here since he and his Kitten have gone off to England for a few weeks. He's offered me the apartment to stay in while he's gone in exchange for my assistance to Mason in running the club. But with my job at the Parker residence, I was sleeping on the sofa rather than the pool house I was offered. All because I wanted to be close, making sure Madison was safe.

Even though I've paid rent on my own place, I've hardly been there. A waste really, but I didn't want to leave Madison on her own.

The elevator takes me up to the penthouse floor, and when the metal doors slide open, I step out into the hallway. There are two apartments here, one on the west wing of the building and one on the east. My brother has one and Mason, his business partner, has the other.

Once I'm inside the living room, I shrug off my jacket, hanging it on the back of the living room chair. When I walked out of the house two days ago, I made a choice that I'll never go back. Though I know I'm lying to myself.

I've never wanted a woman's approval before. Never needed her to feel something for me, something that I myself am struggling to understand. But with her, it's different. I want to protect her as much as I want to hurt her.

My fist meets the brick wall beside the door in a moment of fury and frustration. She's fucking marrying him. Her father is forcing her into a loveless fucking marriage, and I can't do shit about it. But then again, I'm an O'Leary, and one thing I've learned is we do not sit back and let something fall through our fingers. No. This time, I'll fight.

She looks at me like maybe I'm a real man. Not a trained killer. Not someone who's tortured people, but someone she could perhaps see forever with. It makes me sound weak. My father told me from a young age, affection, love more importantly, can make a grown man fall to his knees.

I vowed to never fall. To never kneel. But I lied again. Because I have fallen. For the sweet brunette who's now alone because I'm no good for her. She deserves better than me.

Nothing's made sense since she walked into my life. Since I got a taste of her, I've become someone I don't recognize. When I first thrust my cock into Madison, I knew I'd never be the same again.

I may not have wanted love, but it knocked my fucking door down.

For a long time, I wasn't even sure I would ever know what love was.

And to be honest, I don't want to just love her.

I want to fucking own her.

My phone rings in my jacket pocket, dragging me from thoughts of the sweet woman I need more than my next breath. Once I have the device, I note the name on screen.

Oliver.

"Hey," I answer immediately.

"I have something for you. The young man working with Magnus, his name is—"

"Hudson?" I finish his sentence, interrupting him mid-speech.

"Yeah, he's just left the lake house you told me about. I have him on tracker. He's headed to a motel not far, actually. I can get the coordinates to you," he informs me of something I've been waiting for. The asshole is going to pay.

"Get it to me."

"Callan," Oliver says my name in warning, and I know what's coming next. "Don't do anything stupid."

"Come on, man, this is me you're talking to. I never do stupid shit." I chuckle, but I'm anything but calm right now.

"If you're anything like your brother, I don't believe that for a second," he says. A deep rumble comes from the other end of the line. "Take care."

With that, he hangs up, and a moment later, my phone is beeping with the intel he's promised. Hudson is meeting someone, perhaps his father, maybe Madison's father, but I'm going to get to the bottom of this fucking arranged marriage.

I've been here for fifteen minutes with no action. It's dark, the lights in the room of the block of apartments are off. I thought it was a motel, but when I arrived, I noted it's been turned into cheap housing.

My gaze is drawn back to a light flicking on in

an apartment on the second floor. The old brick-face building is almost falling apart, but when a man appears at the window, I'm not surprised at all. Mr. Parker is in the bedroom. I watch him turn to face a woman with blonde hair. From here, I can't make out her face, but she looks young. Perhaps he's with a high-class hooker. But then she turns toward the window, and I recognize her as the same blonde from the last time I recorded Magnus.

There's no mistaking it's her.

Madison's best friend.

Amber Davenport.

Another person moves in the apartment. He steps up behind the young blonde, and I'm surprised that it's not, in fact, Hudson in the apartment with him—it's Mr. Brockovich himself. Gregory is standing back, his eyes on the scene I'm afforded, along with a smirk on his face. Both men have cigars, and I wonder how much they've already had to drink.

Magnus Parker's hands cup her pert ass cheeks, gripping them after he swats her playfully on both fleshy globes. They move into the bedroom, and my gaze trails along with them. It's light enough to see her body straddle Brockovich's, and my mind drifts to the beautiful Madison Parker. Picturing her straddling me has my cock rage behind my metal zipper.

When I walked out on her, I didn't want to leave, but I knew I had to. Keeping her safe was at the forefront of my mind. I've never cared for anyone besides my family. But the thought of her being hurt by this asshole set my body on edge.

I know I let my feelings get in the way. I should never have fucked her, tasted her. But I did, and now I wonder if there's a way she'll forgive me for leaving, if not I won't blame her.

A soft vibration sounds beside me, and I wonder if it's her, but then I remember I was expecting a call. "Oliver," I answer after glancing at his name flashing on the screen.

"How are you doing, Callan?" he says from the other end of the line, and I can hear the smirk in his tone.

"The usual, watching and waiting . . ." I allow my words to trail off.

"Like a venom," he responds. Men have said I'm akin to a poison, because when I kill, it's slow and meticulous.

"And he's there?"

I shake my head. "Not him, but this is even better. It's his dad and Magnus. And they're getting their rocks off with a Amber Davenport, Madison's so-called best friend."

He chuckles over the line, already knowing what's going on. "Perfect. Don't forget to send me the footage."

When Oliver mentioned he'd found Hudson, I jumped at the chance to watch this asshole fuck up everything he wants. But now I have so much more to bring down the corrupt Magnus Parker and Gregory Brockovich. Madison will not be marrying Hudson.

She's mine. The thought comes out of nowhere, slamming me right in the chest.

"I'll get it through to you when I get home. I doubt either of them will last very long," I inform the man who's offered me a chance to use the skills I've honed over the years.

"This will be done sooner than we expected. Once the video is leaked, Madison's father will be locked up, and you get your girl," he says with satisfaction in his tone.

"I don't doubt that, Oliver." The line dies, and I know he's possibly chuckling to himself.

When I first met Oliver, I knew he'd be a good contact to have. When Carrick told me about the work Mr. Michaelson needed done, I knew Oli was the man to talk to, and I offered my services. He jumped at the chance to hire me. He may work in one of the most well-known insurance firms in the city, but it's his other business that keeps him living the lifestyle he enjoys so much.

After chucking my phone on the seat beside me, my gaze travels back to the window where I'm glued to the scene before me. Madison doesn't deserve this, her father is a lying scumbag, her so-called best friend is a whore, and she's meant to be marrying into a family that's just as vile. She's nothing like her father.

No.

Madison is a woman who's been broken. Shattered. But somehow, I've managed to draw out the real her. The one she hides. Her little cunt drips when she's ordered to come for me, and when her pretty, smooth lips are slapped hard. Her body trembles with need when she's bound and whipped, the more intense the better. Her need for pain is something I've grown to love about her. And soon, I'll give her exactly what she desires.

Watching the two men I want to slaughter with my blade fuck a girl that's young enough to be their daughter. This is the first time that Magnus has had his friend with him, and I wonder how much damage it will do to both their names. Each time I've caught the evidence we need that Magnus is a corrupt piece of shite, I've realize how badly I need Madison away from him. Away from her own father.

I think about how much I know about her and the secrets she hides from everyone. Her pain, her past, those scars that make her even more beautiful. All the things I should've told her but didn't because I'm an asshole.

I start the engine and pull out into the road. As I head toward the lake house, thoughts of her are running rife through my mind. When I'd arrived with my sister and when Rick told me I had free reign in his club, I delved into the world I'd only had a taste of back in England.

But the night I took Madison Parker with her big eyes that shimmered with restrained hunger, she spun my world deep into the abyss. She reveled in the danger, the sweet punishments and pain.

The moment I pulled out the metal instrument, she didn't shy away. No, my little flower, with more thorns than petals, pleaded for more. She challenged me every step of the way, and that's what I did. I gave it to her, and I have finally met my match. A woman who can tame me yet turn me into a monster at the same time.

I recall the hypnotic moans and mewls that fell from her mouth. How her lips parted on gasps of pleasure. And that's the moment I knew I'd be addicted to her forever. The way her back arched, the slope of her breasts, the rosy nipples that hardened at my cool touch, and her keening cries made me harder than I've ever been.

I held onto the cool metal of the weapon in my hand as if it were my lifeline. Perhaps it was that night. But my need to kill is there, to wipe Hudson's smug face from this earth so he can never go near my woman again. Maybe I'll never change. I've tried. For her, I did give it my best shot, but even she can't temper the beast hiding within me.

I crave that power, of having someone beg for their life. Especially when they don't deserve to be alive. That's what I want, to snuff out that light and watch it slowly dim until they take their last breath.

It's become an addiction over the years, and it's led me on a darkened path I can't bring myself to come back from. The constant need and hunger to be high, to feel that intensity shooting through your bloodstream. The tingle over bare skin. The thrum of your heart when you know you're about to get everything you've been edging toward.

And finally, bliss as you dive from the precipice and immerse yourself in the abyss of pleasure. Of the high.

TWENTY

MADISON

The lake is dark, almost as if it's a piece of glass that could shatter at any time. I feel as if I'm close to shattering. As if I can break as soon as I hear the door click behind me. Hudson called an hour ago telling me he'll be here tonight. As much as I hate him, he seemed to be taking to the idea of the wedding far-too well.

"I'm out here," I call to him.

"I know." The voice that comes from behind me isn't Hudson's, which causes me to leap to my feet. When I find *him* standing in the doorway, I want to run up and leap into his arms, but I don't. I'm still angry.

"What are you doing here?"

He smirks, pushing off the door frame. "Well," he starts, closing the distance between us easily with a few steps. "I wanted to come and see the pretty bride to be." His voice is tainted with fury. It's so harsh it trickles over me, making me shiver.

"You don't get to do this, Callan," I tell him, folding my arms in front of my chest, which draws his eyes to my breasts.

"Do what, Blossom?" he questions softly, his voice dripping desire. His hands are on my hips, pulling me closer. "This?" he asks. Leaning in, he plants a soft kiss on my check. "Or this?" He trails his tongue over my cheek lightly. "Or was it this?" he questions as he finds my neck, suckling the sensitive flesh into his mouth, his teeth biting down as he asserts the way he's assaulting my flesh, and even though I should stop him, I don't want to.

His fingers dig into my hips, his cock pressing against my stomach, warning me of the thickness hiding behind his zipper. His body is taut with restraint. My hands land on his shoulders, and he visibly ripples with it. He needs this as much as I do.

"Callan, please," I whimper, and that's all he needs to lift me by my hips and carry me to the bedroom. All the way up the stairs, he kisses me. Our mouths fused, our tongues duel and dance as he owns me once more.

When we reach the room, he sets me down on the bed, his body still nestled between my thighs, his hands on either side of my head. And there's something in his eyes telling me so much more than any words he can offer.

"Why did you come here?" My question stills him for a moment. He presses his hips against me, allowing his cock against my clit to send a jolt of pleasure through me.

"You're mine." Two words whispered to me in the dark make me smile. "I came here to make sure you remember no matter who's in your bed." He leans in and plants a soft kiss on my pouty lips. "I'm the one who can make you scream for god."

"You can't just walk in here and expect me to forgive you for leaving. You left without an explanation, Callan. I didn't know if you were dead or not. I needed you." My words are far too fragile for this moment, and he sees it. He sees how broken I am.

"I needed you safe. My life — Fuck, there's so

much wrong in my life. I've spent this time fighting a war, hoping my princess is safe." There's a sweetness in his words that breaks through my anger. "I'm no knight, Madison, and there's no doubt I'll never be a prince, but I can keep you safe from a distance."

"I don't want you at a distance," I tell him earnestly. I wish he'd see that without him I'm worse off. I don't know why. I can't explain our connection, but it's there. It always has been.

"Then I'll be right here, for tonight. I can't promise you forever, Madison. I told you that before. I'm not ready for hearts-and-flowers shit."

"Such a romantic," I sass him, earning me a gentle chuckle.

"I'll show you romantic," he tells me. Rising to full height, he pulls out a thin strip of material from his jacket pocket, a pair of cuffs that were hidden on the waistband of his black jeans, and his sleek silver blade. "Lie back, baby girl. Tonight, I'm claiming what's mine."

"Hudson will be here soon," I inform him, but the look on his face tells me I'm wrong. He's done something. "What did you do?" I move back onto the bed, my head on the pillows.

"He's rather tied up at the moment," he responds with a wink then proceeds in tying my wrists to the posts on either side of the headboard. My legs are bound open to the wooden frame foot-end of the bed. When he's done, he steps back to admire me from where he's standing. "Perfect."

The small pair of shorts I was wearing, and the slinky material of my panties are sliced from my body along with my tank top. I'm bared to him once more, and I wonder if he can see my soul crying out for this, for him.

From the inner part of his dark jacket, he pulls out a long, slim strip of leather, and I note it's a whip. It's coiled like a serpent, and when he grips the handle and releases the long tongue, it whooshes in the air. He shrugs his jacket off and tugs the T-shirt he's wearing from the waistband of his jeans.

"Are you ready to play?"

"Yes, Callan." I whimper when he brings the whip down over my thighs. Again and again. Over the marks I've hidden for so long. His gaze burns into me, past those silver reminders of my past. He turns my skin red, and I revel in it. My hips lift when the fine point of the leather nips at where my clit is hidden by my panties, causing me to cry out in agonizing pleasure.

"Please. Oh, god, please," I beg, pleading with him to fuck me, make me come. Anything. It's torture being away from him, but being near him and not feeling his hands on me is driving me insane.

"Did you fuck him?" he asks as he continues his assault on my legs, shins, my stomach. "Did you, Madison?"

"No!" I shriek when it hits my nipple, the hardened bud throbbing as he smirks down at me. After the lashings, he sets the whip down and shoves his shoes off. Then with one hand, pulls his tee up and over his head, and I'm met with the glorious view of his toned torso, his tanned skin, and the thick bulge in his now open jeans. The zipper is low, and his pants hang from his tapered hips.

He crawls over me, hovering above me like a hunter about to attack its prey. He uses his knife and trails it over and around my nipple, the rosy color darkening and puckering against the cold metal.

"So pretty," he says in awe, copying the action with my other breast. "All day, all night, every fucking hour of the day, Madison," he grunts, then lifts his gaze to mine. The sharp tip of the blade under my chin. "I think about you, about your smile, your eyes, I fantasize about your pretty little cunt and how tight it is around my dick."

The filthy words he's offering only intensifies the ache between my legs. My skin is tingling from my whipping, my clit throbbing for attention.

"And you know what I do?" he says, leaning in, pulling a nipple into his mouth and sucking on it harshly. Tugging it between his teeth, then laving at it with his tongue. He tortures me like this for what feels like hours.

He lifts his gaze to mine. "I fist my cock. I stroke it slowly," he tells me, and by the time his mouth moves lower, over my bare stomach to my belly button, I'm a puddle of arousal just waiting for him to drink me in.

"Callan, please," I beg shamelessly. My legs splayed, I'm open. I can smell myself.

"You're so wet, Blossom," he smirks. "Is my pretty

flower wanting to be plucked and devoured?" He uses the knife in his hand to trail along my mound, eliciting a whimper and mewl from me. "Look at that beautiful cunt." His gaze is locked on my core, his tongue darting out to lick his lips hungrily. "I want to eat it until you're shaking, then I'm going to fuck you raw. I want you to hurt tomorrow. I want you to remember when *he* walks in here later that I'm the one who fucking owns you."

He drops his head between my thighs, and his mouth goes to work on my body. His tongue fucks me deep as if his cock is driving into me. My toes curl when he sucks my clit into his mouth. With two thick fingers, he dips them into my pussy, crooking them to press against the sweet spot inside me that sets the fireworks off. They shoot behind my eyelids as I cry out in pleasure.

My hips rock against his face. I'm fucking myself on his mouth, and all I can think of is more. I need it. I want it. He doesn't relent. His lips close around my smooth lips, and he drinks me like I'm his favorite beverage. His fingers tease my back entrance, swirling around it with my arousal, and when his finger slips into the tight ring of muscle, I find another release, soaking Callan's mouth, chin, and coating his tongue in my juices.

I'm nowhere near coming down from my high when I feel him at my pussy. His cock gently nudging me open. "Look, Madison," he tells me.

I open my eyes and find the sight of his cock against the lips of my pussy too much, and I moan loudly. "Please, Callan, just fuck me."

"Watch how my big cock splits your pretty petals. Look how I break my Blossom." He's growling like a rabid dog as he inches into me. Once he's fully seated, he doesn't move for a moment, and then, before I have time to say anything, he pulls out and drives back in, causing my body to slide up the bed.

He reaches for my neck, gripping me tightly, and my body pulses with need. "You love my fingers wrapped around your throat. Don't you, Blossom?" he grits out through clenched teeth. "You see, Madison, you're breathless and vulnerable."

I want to claw at his wrist, to dig my nails into the flesh, igniting dark desire inside him, but I can't. Instead, I nod as I lift my hips, begging wordlessly for more.

"You're mine." Two words have me whimpering

as tears form in my eyes when I realize it's true. I see it in his eyes. He loves me. He can't say it, but he doesn't need to. It's written all over his face. His expression tells me everything I need to know.

We move in sync.

Our hips slam against each other.

His hands on my hips, holding me in place as he fucks me into the mattress.

There's an overflow of love here, but we're not sweet and gentle. There's nothing more than two people who need each other to be whole. And when we're connected, with him inside my like this, I'm me.

Finally.

"Fuck, you feel so good," he utters into my neck, his mouth latching on as he ruts like an animal that's just lost all control.

"I want to come. I want you to fill me, Callan, please." Words fall from my mouth. My wrists ache, my ankles protest, but when I roll my hips and squeeze myself around him, I draw his orgasm as mine suddenly slams into me, and I call his name again.

I chant it. It's my prayer.

He's my savior.

And my sin.

TWENTY-ONE

CALLAN

My body is still tense from seeing her. I laid my claim. She knows she's mine, and as much as her father doesn't approve, there's no fucking denying it. I left her in bed, her body draped in the soft, white sheet. One of the most difficult things I've ever had to do.

But when my phone vibrated beside the bed where I was holding onto Madison like she was my lifeline, I knew. I got the message from Oliver there's an urgent meeting this morning at the Parker residence. Mr. Oliver Michaelson, a man who wears many caps, one being his law degree, has been called in to help.

The video leaked this morning. As soon as Magnus Parker's PR saw it, they sent a request of removal, but if there's one thing I've learned over the years, once it's on the internet and gone viral, there's no way of unseeing it.

I can't help chuckling at the thought of Magnus crumbling to his knees, begging for Oliver's help. A man on his knees shows his weakness — that's what my father used to tell me. But when I'm with Madison, I'll gladly show her my weakness because she makes me want to show her my soul.

I've been a bad man all my life. I don't deny I am. But I'll spend the rest of my days changing that to make her smile. To have the love of Madison Parker is a gift I don't feel worthy of, but she gives it anyway.

The sun is just rising on the horizon, the sky turning from the darkness of night to the soft hues of day. Last night is playing on my mind. Those tender moments, along with the rough, have burrowed themselves in my heart. It was the moment Madison begged me to fill her — I found in that moment I did want to. The idea of her pregnant with my child brings out the caveman in me.

I thought I could walk away, I thought I could leave her after one taste, but it's not satiated my hunger. No, I need her beneath and beside me forever. I want to hear her cry. To watch her porcelain skin welt with red when I whip her into submission.

Don't get me wrong. I want nothing more than to have her by my side as my partner, but in the bedroom, she'll be on her knees as my equal, because God knows that woman is strong and resilient.

First though, I have to find out what her father is planning to do now that his seat has been threatened by his extracurricular activities. I can't be in the meeting with them, but Oliver has given me a way in without them knowing. As I pull up to the rear of the mansion, I set the car in park and wait.

My thoughts drift back to my girl in bed this morning. Leaving her was difficult, but I made it back to the city with time to spare. Now, as I sit here with my phone burning a hole in my pocket, I watch my mark pull up to Magnus's property. Hudson Brockovich, the asshole who wants to fuck me over by hurting Madison. I know he will. There's an iciness in the way he looked at me, one of a killer.

It reminds me of who I was. And yes, right now, I realize why Carrick stopped working for our father. I know now why he wanted an out. I recall the moment he took his revenge. It was only a few months ago now, but it feels like yesterday. The only thing is, he doesn't know what really happened that day, and I don't intend to tell him either.

I should've done it. I should've told my brother to stay home while I exact the revenge he's been wanting for so long, but I know if I'd have done that, he would never get the closure he needs.

The sun is low on the horizon as we make our way up to the house. The building is old, but it's warning of darkened windows tells us to stay away. My brother, however, has never been one for rules or someone telling him what to do.

I follow him toward the door, my steps right behind his. Watching his back has been my life's work. I've always been there for him, and I wouldn't have it any other way.

When I glance up, I note the man we've come here for in the window. He sees us. He knows us. We move to the door, which opens before Carrick can knock. A woman regards us warily as if we're the bad guys. If only she knew she was in the same house as the devil.

"Hello," she says quietly. There's an Irish lilt in her voice, and I recognize it as a Northern accent. She knows who

we are, and I wonder if he's warned her. If he told her why we're here. She doesn't look scared, but there's a flit in her gaze that tells me she's been waiting to open the door to us.

We move inside, and already the tension in the space is enough to fucking choke us to death. Wouldn't he enjoy that? But today this asshole is not taking anything else from the O'Learys.

"Carrick Aiden O'Leary." When he uses Rick's full name, there's a thick accent behind his words, one that reminds me of days at home. When I was knee-deep in blood and guts after killing the men who wronged us.

I know why my brother walked out. I understood it. But deep down, I know that will never be me. I can never walk away. I have no reason to.

"Seamus Moran," Carrick says, and the man watches us. I'm hyperaware of the silence in the house, there's more to this meeting than we can both see, and I have a feeling shit is about to hit the fan.

I pull out my phone, recording the meeting for our father. The confession of our sworn enemy is something that will please him.

When Moran offers me a seat, I pin him with a hateful

glare. There's no way I want to stay here longer than is needed. My weapon is ready in the holster, and I know I'm going to need it.

Call it instinct, but I feel it trickle over me, as if warning me.

"I've come to make sure you pay your dues," Carrick says in a tone dripping with confidence. I've seen my brother kill before. I've watched him torture people, but I know it's not him.

Moran doesn't say anything. He gestures instead with his hands for Carrick to do as he wishes because he knows the way we live. The code we follow. I can't draw my gaze away from my brother pulling the trigger. The resounding shot hits the asshole in the knee, but it's not the sound that makes me step closer to the scene and shove my phone in my pocket.

It's the flinch in my brother's expression that tells me he's not going to be able to do this. And like so many times before, I'll help my younger brother.

The second bullet hits Moran's other kneecap, and his grip on the oozing wounds is almost comical. Four men appear, and my heart kicks against my ribs. This is going down.

My hand is on my gun. The grip is white knuckled as I

watch my brother, then I land my eyes on the men in the room. The slightest movement and I'll kill the fucking lot of them.

"They say cockroaches never learn. They never die either, but I'm here to ensure that you're on the path straight to hell, Moran," Carrick bites out angrily.

"As you know the code we live by, O'Leary. An eye for an eye. This is done. The men behind me will escort you from this house, and I suggest you stay away. I'll move on, back to Ireland, but you're not to follow. Your father will know I've paid with my legs."

"You fucking took her from me!" My brother's tone is filled with anguish, and I feel it down to the marrow in my bones. He's on his feet, making a move against Moran when the men flanking the asshole cock their guns, but Seamus stops them.

Anger fuels Carrick as he drags Moran to the sofa. Their faces inches apart. I'm not sure what he's doing, but he grits out, "You killed her." He rains down punch after punch on the man's face, and I know he's lost in the anger. There's crunching of a bone. Blood drenches him, and Seamus is almost limp when Carrick finally stops. He's crying. I've never seen my brother cry. Not even when Aurora was murdered.

I help him to stand. Leaning in, I whisper to him, hoping to get past that wall he's put up in anger. "It's done, brother. We need to leave."

"Remember, O'Leary, there's always a time and place for everything. You've gotten what you came for. If you ever come near me again, I'll ensure you don't walk out the door."

We're almost at the door when Rick turns to me. "Callan, wait outside." There's a plea in his gaze, and I nod. He might be younger, and lower in rank than I am, but I know he needs this.

There's one shot, just one, and then chaos seems to erupt with a loud crack. I can't leave him in there. My body is moving swiftly as I race back indoors, my gun already poised and my finger pulling the trigger over and over as I take the men by surprise.

Four dead bodies.

I turn to find Seamus chuckling but slumped on the floor. Carrick must've shot him, but he's not dead. "Your brother has confidence," he tells me. "Do you?"

I glance at my brother who's unconscious, and I know I need to get him to the hospital. There's blood oozing from his shoulder. I meet the cold eyes of Seamus and smirk. "You *fucked with the wrong family," I bite out, pressing the barrel of my gun against his forehead. Point blank. Then pull the trigger.*

The sleek, silver vehicle pulling up to the residence drags me from the memory of me killing Seamus Moran. The asshole deserved it. He should've gotten a far more painful death, but I couldn't do much more with Carrick there. He needed the hospital, and I wasn't about to let my brother die.

It's always been about family. There was never a time I didn't do something that wasn't for any one of them. When Carrick left, I was there for my father and sister, but deep down I knew I'd bring them all together again. And I hope when this shit is over, the event that will bring us all together is a wedding.

My phone rings loudly, and I swipe the screen. Oliver's told me to keep my phone on hand so when he calls I can listen to the conversation without anyone knowing I'm there.

"This is fucking ridiculous. I asked for it to be removed." Madison's father is panicked. I can tell from the tone in his voice.

"I understand your concerns, Mr. Parker." Oliver's smooth tone is unfazed by the manic old man who's been paying to get his dick wet.

"I'm paying you an extortionate rate. If you can't get it taken down, I'll find someone who can," Magnus hisses angrily, and I can picture just how tense he is. Another call comes through, and I see her pretty face blinking at me, but I can't answer. Not just yet. I need to wait until Oliver is done.

I ignore the call, hoping she won't be too angry with me.

I'll be back for you soon, baby.

"My fucking daughter is planning a wedding!" The shrill voice comes back, drawing me to the present and right to the violent urge to rip his heart from his chest. The fact that he's forcing his daughter to marry an asshole like Hudson Brockovich is beyond me.

The second call comes through. I want to answer her, to respond, but I can't.

"I want that O'Leary brought in. I asked him to look after my daughter, and he goes MIA. Find him and get him here."

"Sir, I don't think—"

"I don't fucking pay you to think!"

"Mr. Parker," Oliver says, attempting to placate the man in his cool yet confident tone, but Magnus is beyond fucking hysterical. "I understand you're panicking. I've already been on the phone with your public relations team. They've got the videos down, but you have to realize, it went viral within ten minutes of being uploaded."

"If my daughter sees that," Magnus responds, and finally I hear a hint of regret in his voice. I wonder if he really has found a conscience. "She'll be lost to me forever."

"I understand your concern, but you have to realize that what you were doing in that video is detrimental. If someone looks into it, if they find the woman you were with and she testifies about what happened between you . . ." Oliver allows the words to sink in.

"Mr. Parker." Hudson's voice comes across the line, and my blood is boiling just at the smug tone. "I'll go to Madi. I'll keep her at the lake house until this has calmed down somewhat." *Like fuck, you will.*

"Thank you, Hudson. You're a good boy."

Before he has time to get to his car, I'm already starting the engine and pulling out onto the road. I'll get to her before he does. Oliver can wait until I've got my girl, and we'll meet at his house later. There's no way in hell I'm allowing Hudson anywhere near Madison.

Not now.

Not ever.

TWENTY-TWO

MADISON

Thump. Thump. Thump.

I feel it. Feel him.

When I woke up, he was gone. I'd called twice, and he didn't respond. I'm not sure where Callan went, but my post bliss was gone, and panic was setting in. And then Hudson strolled in. I'm not sure what he gave me, but my body is boneless. I can't move as I lean against the cabinet in the bathroom.

I want to run, but I can't leave. My father sent a message telling me the wedding has been moved up to tomorrow, and that's when Hudson wandered into the bedroom, holding me down as he injected me with something. Anger fizzled into sadness then into fear. My heart aches for the man I've grown to love, and now I'm here, stuck with a man I hate.

There's no way for me to get out of here. I have no driver or car. The two men who were watching the lake house have left, and I'm alone with someone who's trying to hurt me, and I'm fearful that he'll get it right.

It's far too quiet. I don't know where he went, not even a sound comes from the kitchen which makes me wonder what's going to happen to me. I'm alone with my thoughts. The memories both steal my breath and hurt my heart. The memories of last night with Callan are forever emblazoned in me.

Like a scar. A tattoo that will last long after I take my final breath.

He wasn't here to love me. He made me cry and scream.

But it was his ruthlessness that made me fall for him.

I glance down at the ruby color on my thighs. And for the first time in my life, I'm not the one who's done it.

I've been so strong, but now that I watch the open cuts drip, I allow it to release the pain in my chest. Long ago, before I'd attempted to do it, I read about the act of cutting. Had seen the horrific images on the internet, but it didn't stop me. At thirteen I still took a razor blade to my flesh and watched as the deep-red liquid trickled from my wounds.

It was a release.

I felt as if all the bad things that happened to me were finally being expunged, and I got addicted to the feeling. The same way a drug addict or alcoholic feels when they shoot up or take a drink. It's scary how much you need it, crave it. Since I was young, I've found release in it. I was okay when I'd woken up with Callan gone only an hour ago. I thought perhaps he was just out at the store, or something. But Hudson arrived and dragged me in here, then took a blade to my thighs.

I've struggled all my life with the pain inside. When Callan was around, I forgot about it, pushed it aside. But with him gone now, and Hudson here, I think my father had something to do with it. I've learned one thing about Daddy — whatever he wants, he gets. I glance at my phone which was hidden in the pocket of my shorts, pressing send on the message to Callan. It may be the last one I ever get to him.

A tear trickles its way down my cheek. I hear the door. And then the footsteps.

It's Hudson, and he's here to finish what he started. He's wanted everything my father has for so long, and now he's taking it, piece by piece.

The depression clouds around me. I feel it again, niggling away at me. Wanting to be let out, to drip from my skin. My sadness stemmed from a childhood of being bullied, from parents who didn't care, and from a mother who walked out. Left before I had time to even know her. Some people may think it's an excuse. They look at me and wonder how someone who's had everything her heart could desire could ever feel like I do. But material things don't offer solace. They don't hold you when you're scared.

But Callan did.

He somehow mended those shattered pieces of me.

With his rough exterior, harsh commands, and his gentle soul, he hid behind high walls, I felt whole for the first time in a long while. I've never allowed anyone to get close enough to give something of myself. But he saw it. He filtered through my words, my smiles and sass, and he found the girl beneath.

Somehow, in our differences, we fit perfectly. His jagged edges with my soft curves. It's as if he slotted himself inside me, and now, I'll never rid myself of him.

It's been a long while since I sat in this position on my bathroom floor. When I finally went for help, I didn't think I'd ever find myself here again, but the pain has returned. He's the one who walked out, and I let him. I told him to leave, and he did.

What did I expect?

The silver glints at me. It reminds me of the high. The freedom from pain.

"What the fuck are you doing?" Hudson hisses when he sees my phone on the floor beside me. "You're a stupid little bitch just like Amber warned me." His hate-fueled words swirl around me. I feel drunk, drugged, my limbs are limp, and I can no longer move them. There are hands on me, but I'm weak. I can't fight him this time. He drags me by my arms to the bedroom. Lifting me easily, Hudson places me on the bed.

"Amber," I whimper when he leaves me and heads

back to the bathroom. I'm confused. What is he talking about?

When he returns, he's carrying the blade he had earlier. "You see, I've been fucking your beautiful blonde friend for years." His words slice into me like the razor blade itself, the pain acute. It's his tone, that vicious anger, that hurts me. I don't care about Hudson, but deep down, that teenage girl who wanted to be beautiful like the other girls rears her head.

"Why are you doing this?"

He smirks. Moving onto the bed, he straddles me, pressing me into the mattress. Hudson lifts my arm, pushing the blade into my wrist, and I can't help wincing.

"Don't you like this?" he questions, and I watch in horror as he slices into the caramel flesh of my wrist.

"No, please! Hudson," I cry out, but it's no use. I try to punch him, to shake him off like I learned in self-defense classes, but he's learned my moves. And I can't shake him. His fist connects to my face so painfully I cry out in agony.

"You see," he starts, "when they find your lifeless

body, nobody will care, because you did this to yourself."
He informs me of this confidently. And he's right. I've
been doing this for far too long to hide it, and he knows
it. He knew it all along.

My head is spinning from the loss of blood and
the harsh attack from his large fist. "Please." My voice
sounds weaker than I want it to. The clothes I'm wearing
are turning red from the blood dripping onto me. He
grips my neck, tightening his hold on me, and I can feel
my lungs protest.

"Fuck, you look so pretty all broken. I should've
done this a long time ago. At least Amber lets me have
my way with her," Hudson hisses. His hips undulate
above me, his erection pressing into my body. My
stomach convulses as he jerks himself off against me.

"Stop. Please?"

"One more time? For old time's sake," he says,
ripping my tank top open, exposing my breasts. My
panties soon follow, and he's pushing my thighs apart.
I'm not ready. My body is not responding, but he doesn't
notice.

I feel him nudge my entrance. "Please, no. No,

Hudson!" I cry out when he drives into my dry core, and it feels like I'm ripped apart.

"You're so tight, Madicakes," he coos in my ear. My stomach rolls with revulsion. He's kneeling, lifting my hips against him so his hands are free to maul my breasts. He tugs and pulls on my nipples. The blood from my wrist is no longer trickling—it's rushing from the wound.

"Please," I whimper, attempting to stop the bleeding, but Hudson rips my left hand away.

"I'll cut both," he warns. "Then I'll make you come all over my cock like the little whore you are. Does it get you off?" he questions. "Cutting your flesh? Because fuck, your pretty ruby blood is making me hard."

"Stop. Hudson." My voice is hoarse, and I'm slowly losing consciousness. My eyes flutter as he continues to violate me. The thickness of him inside my dry channel bring tears to my eyes.

The light is gone. My eyes are closed. I think. I can hear him. The grunting. There's pain in my stomach. I'm not sure what it is, but it hurts. I can't open my eyes. He finally releases my neck, but I can't pull in air.

I gasp, but it's not helping.

"Goodbye, Madicakes. I couldn't come inside you, or they'd know I was here," he laughs. Evil. Sadistic. And then I'm alone.

TWENTY-THREE

CALLAN

Pulling up to the cabin, I curse as I push my door open and race up to the house. I had to pull over to take an emergency call from Oliver, but I don't see another car anywhere in the vicinity, so I've still beat Hudson here. Thank fuck.

The silence that greets me when I shove the door open is ghostly.

"Madison!" I call out as I make my way through the living room, into the kitchen, but there's nobody downstairs. Perhaps she's still sleeping. I take the steps two at a time and shove into the bedroom where I'd taken her again and again last night.

The sight that meets me knocks the breath from my lungs. Her naked body is lying in crimson sheets.

"Baby, fuck," I curse loudly, as I rip the sheet apart. The flimsy material tears easily. Quickly, I wrap her arm up to stop the blood loss. Then I cocoon her in the blanket that's been folded neatly on the chair beside the bed. Her body is so cold, and I wonder just how fucking long she's been like this. *Why would she do this?*

There's a blade beside her — small and silver — underneath her ruby-colored life force. Anger courses through my veins when I think about her doing shit like this. I've never felt this kind of rage before.

"Hold on. Please, just fucking hold on," I tell her as I make my way down to the car. Leaving the house unlocked, I place her on the back seat, keeping her hidden in the blanket. I don't know how much blood she's lost, but I need to get her to the hospital.

My heart aches. It feels as if it's been carved from my fucking chest.

Hitting dial on my phone, I wait for Oliver to answer. On the third ring, his voice comes from the other end. "Callan."

"I need you to call in your contacts at the hospital. It's an emergency."

"Why? What's wrong?"

"It's Madison. I found her bleeding out on the bed in the lake house. I'm not sure what the fuck happened, but she's unconscious."

"Fuck," his hiss comes across loud and clear. "I'll ensure they know you're on your way. Dr. Harlow will be waiting at Chicago Gen," he tells me then hangs up. My lungs feel as if they're not pulling in enough air.

I've seen blood. I've fucking caused so many deaths, but this is far too much for me to handle. It's surreal. I wanted my girl, I finally found her, and I can't fucking lose her.

"Madison fucking Parker, don't you dare die on me," I warn her, even though I know she can't hear me. My foot is flat on the gas pedal, my body thrumming with anxiety. It's not too far, but timing is critical.

And as I weave through the traffic, I do something I haven't done in a long while.

I pray.

I fucking pray to a God who has long since forgotten me because of all the things I've done. Since I turned sixteen, I've walked the dark path my father led me on.

He didn't force it on me; I walked willingly. I followed him, and I wanted everything the life offered.

"Callan," my father's rough voice comes from the doorway.

When I turn around, I find him holding a sleek, silver gun. I don't know much about them, but from watching the men who work for us, I've noted a few things about how they're held, how to load one, but I can't for the life of me tell you what the name is or what caliber it is either.

One day though.

I'll learn.

"I need ye with me right now, son," my father huffs, turning to leave only for me to traipse behind him. I'm the eldest by one year. Carrick, my younger brother, and Cayleigh, our little sister are nowhere to be found, and I wonder if he's sent them into town.

When he has the men here for meetings, he sends them away so they don't have to watch what's happening. My brother only being fifteen is too young to be in this life. And our sister, who's seven, certainly shouldn't be around the goons my father employs.

As soon as we round the corner and step into the garage, the stale scent of blood assaults my nose. The metallic smell is heavy, as if it's a cloud consuming me.

"What is going on?" My question goes unanswered.

"This." My father gestures to the man seated on the chair before me. He's bloodied and beaten, bound with metal cuffs to the chair. His once white teeth are broken and red with ruby-colored, metallic liquid. "Is a man who was stealing from us."

I glance at my father, then back at the thief. Anger surges through me at the news of what this asshole was doing. He deserves being beaten.

"I trust you're ready for this, Callan?" My father's voice is steady as he hands me the heavy metal gun. My eyes fall to the weapon, then raise up to the eyes that match my brother's. Deep golden orbs.

"I'm ready," I inform him.

"Good boy," he tells me. "Remember, always be ruthless."

His words echo as I lift the gun and aim it at the man's forehead.

Ruthless.

I smile when I pull the trigger and watch his head slump forward.

This is what I've wanted for so long, for my father to be proud of me. And when I turn to face him, I see it. He is proud.

But now, with my girl on the back seat close to death, I want something else. I want something so much more. I want the one thing I never knew I'd ever want or need.

I want love.

I only want it with her.

As soon as I pull up to the hospital, I'm out of the car in seconds. Racing to the back, I jerk open the door, gently lifting my girl in my arms. Not bothering to lock the car, I head into the emergency department.

"Dr. Harlow," I tell the nurse who glances up as I hastily walk through the doors.

"He'll be here in a moment," she says, punching something into the computer keyboard. "Can you tell me the patient's name?"

"Madison Parker," I inform her, and I don't miss the raised eyebrows as she continues her insistent tapping.

"I'm Dr. Harlow." A man with a full head of silver hair races toward me with a team of nurses behind him. "Get me a gurney. Let's get this girl up into surgery. I want her hooked up to an IV and monitors immediately. Move!"

I'm following behind them as they make their way through two large double doors.

"We'll call you once we've stabilized her, but we need you to wait out here," the doctor tells me earnestly.

"Don't you dare let her die," I warn, my voice dripping anxiety and fear. I hear it. I've heard fear on my victim's pleas so many times. And now, here I stand, waiting for the woman I love to make it through the next few hours.

"I'll save her," he tells me confidently and disappears along with Madison lying on a steel bed. My body is tight with worry. That dark thought of her not making it niggles at the back of my mind. And as much as I push it away, for some reason, it's not letting up.

I pace back and forth in the waiting area. My mind playing out all the scenarios that could've led to her doing that shit again. *Why would she fucking do that?* I told her I claimed her, that she's mine. Last night was my promise to her.

Nothing makes sense.

There was no reason for her to even think taking her life is worth it. I should've told her I love her. Last night, when I claimed her, I should've asked her to marry me, to spend forever with me.

But my fear overrode the words, and I just fucked her. I made her come on my cock, and I filled her with my own release. Something I've never done with any other woman in my past. I've never trusted anyone enough to let go. To fully give myself.

And now, the one woman I did allow in has gone and fucking mutilated herself for no apparent reason. My phone buzzes in my pocket, and I know it's Oliver.

"What's up?"

"How is she?" he asks.

Sighing, I stop and lean against the wall. I need a fucking cigarette to calm my erratic heart and mind. "She's in surgery, or some shit. The doctor said he'll let me know as soon as she's stable."

"I'm warning you, her father is on the way. Not sure how he found out, but the tracker on his car is on the move."

"Fuck."

I know what that's going to cause. He's going to come here and blame me. And that's something I can't have.

"I'll head out. I don't need to be here when he arrives. Or I might kill the bastard myself." I hang up before Oliver can reprimand me for wanting her father dead, but it's my honest opinion. The asshole angers me.

I head back to the nurse's station, grabbing a blank page from a small notepad and scribble on it. "I need you to call me as soon as she's awake." I push a page with my number toward her. "Please," I beg. I fucking beg. Because I can't take this. Losing her will leave me vulnerable, open to the pain I long since shoved into the back of my mind.

"Yes, sir. I promise, she'll be okay."

I turn, making my way out the door before her father arrives with the press hot on his tail. The first place I want to go is Sins, to drink, to lose myself in a bottle of Jameson. But I don't. I head out to the apartment my brother offered me when I arrived.

All I can do is wait, and that's leaving me antsy. There's one person I look to when I feel the need to kill.

When all I want to do is find Hudson Brockovich and slit his throat, but I need to wait for Oliver, so I head to see my sister.

Even though she's far younger than me, there's still that shred of hope she holds onto. The same hope I lost a long time ago. She gives that to me, that comfort that Madison can't offer right now.

Slipping into the driver's seat of the SUV, I head to Cayleigh in the hope that she can offer me some form of sanity while I lose my mind with worry.

TWENTY-FOUR

OLIVER

If there's one thing I learned over the years of doing business with men like Magnus Parker, it's that they're filled with fear. Those positions they hold, whether in their companies, or government, those are all precarious. And they take those positions and play with them as if they're untouchable.

That's where the problem lies.

Nobody is untouchable.

Many men have come to me when they've fucked up, when they got caught, and even when they knew their life was over. I can only help those willing to help themselves. And I have a feeling Magnus is not one of those men.

Stalking into the hospital, I unbutton my gray

suit jacket as I reach the receptionist counter. "Madison Parker?" I question easily.

The woman trails her gaze over me like so many before. Women are easy to consume. Offer them a smirk, show them confidence, and they're all over you like white on rice.

"Third floor to the left in ICU, sir." She smiles.

I nod. "Thank you." And I'm off toward the elevators. Callan should be here. She's his girl, but when Magnus is on the warpath to find out what happened to his daughter, I think there's a good chance Callan would be taken in for questioning as soon as he stepped foot inside the hospital.

I sent my team to the lake house as soon as Callan told me he'd found Madison hurt. I have a feeling there might be much more to her injuries than meets the eye. While waiting for the results on their sweep, I step out of the elevator and find Mr. Parker pacing the hallway.

"Magnus," I greet, watching his face contort when he sees me.

"Have you heard anything? Please tell me they've found the asshole," he hisses, his voice low and menacing, but he doesn't scare me for shit.

"I have my men working on it, but the cops are already at your lake house. Why do you think Madison would do this?"

He shakes his head, and for the first time in a long while, I see the man lose his cold exterior. "She's always had problems. I mean . . ." He trails off, settling in the chair, but he looks like he's about to fall to his knees. "I just didn't think she was so unhappy."

"Have you thought about other options? Perhaps this wasn't her doing?"

His head snaps up at my assumption. "What?"

"You're a wealthy man. You've just been outed using a girl who is well-known to be your daughter's best friend. Perhaps someone wanted to get back at you," I inform him easily, as if he should've thought about this earlier. He's her goddamn father, and all he wants to see is the worst in his daughter.

"Are you trying to tell me someone tried to kill my daughter?" The vein in his forehead looks like it's about to explode.

Keeping my expression schooled, I nod once. "It's

a suggestion. Once we've got the report from my men, I'll let you know what we've found. Is there anyone you can think of that would want to hurt your daughter?"

He's silent for a moment before he responds. "No, my daughter was the pillar of society. Her friends loved her. Hudson was going to marry her," he insists.

"Marrying someone doesn't always constitute as love," I tell him.

"What are you trying to say? That Hudson had something to do with this? If I'd had to warrant a guess, I would point my finger in the direction of O'Leary," he bites out.

My phone vibrates, chimes, then begins to ring from my pocket. When I pull it out, I note it's one of the men I have working undercover for me.

"Yes," I answer, turning away from Magnus.

"Prints on the door handle and the blade were picked up. Matches that Brockovich boy. Checked out the surveillance. Your boy Hudson was at the house about ten minutes before O'Leary arrived."

The ice that runs through my veins solidifies as I nod in response, and offer him a quick, "Thank you."

I hang up before he can say anything more. Tapping out a message to Callan, I make my way toward the exit. "I'll be back. Stay with your daughter," I tell my client. But as I've only taken two steps toward the exit when the loud shrill beeping of the machines from Madison's room alert the doctor and three nurses at the station right outside.

The energy in the space changes, and when I meet the eyes of my client, I hear the monotonous beep of the machine. That line that should be beeping is now a long droning sound.

I've heard that sound far too often in my line of work. Being an insurance lawyer, most of my clients call me into the hospital when they know someone is about to take their final breath. And this is no different, however, the woman who's flatlining is Callan's girl and I know, if she were mine, I'd want to be here.

"Get me the defibrillator, stat!"

The doctor races toward the room, pushing by Magnus. I can't stay, but I want to.

"We're losing her!"

"What's going on?"

"She's not responding."

My phone rings wildly in my hand, and I glance down at Callan's name flashing at me. He's going to do something stupid. I turn and leave Madison in the hands of the doctors and pray to God they can save her.

TWENTY-FIVE

CALLAN

Silence.

Loneliness.

I've spent so long on my own, not needing or wanting a woman beside me, now that Madison is gone, all I can think of is her. The way her orange blossom perfume used to fill my senses. And how her smile used to crinkle her button nose. I thought I'd miss her body, taking her and fucking her, but that's only one of the smaller things I miss.

It's her affection, that gentle touch, and how much she used to make me feel. I knew when she kissed me it wasn't because she had to. Not because she wanted something in return. No. She spent time with me because she cared.

Love.

Pain.

Loss.

I've been through it all in the months I've known her. At first, all I knew and felt was that agonizing confusion that comes with wanting to completely obliterate someone and finding your heart torn.

Killing came easy to me all my life. I didn't need to think about it. I loved it. Reveling in the cool metal of my weapon. Watching blood drip from the flesh of my enemies, I was sated.

Until her.

It all changed when I tasted love.

I didn't just bask in it, I fucking drowned myself in it. In her. I savored every drop, and with every sip, I became addicted. And all that shattered the moment I saw her lying on the bed, motionless, her body cold to the touch. I broke.

For the first time in my life.

I. Fucking. Broke.

A knock on the door sounds, and I know it's not her. Oliver told me he's on his way, and when I open the door, he's standing there with a look of rage on his features.

"Callan, I need you to focus," are the first words he tells me, and I know something is wrong. So very wrong, I feel it in my veins. "Hudson was the one who hurt Madison." That's what spurs me into action.

My jacket and keys along with my blade are in my grasp in seconds.

"Take me to the asshole, right the fuck now."

The house we pull up to is larger than the Parker residence, and when the security strolls up to the driver's window, he offers a curt nod at Oliver and opens the gates. As we edge our way up the driveway, my body is tense with anger rolling through me.

Hudson's car is parked to the left of the house, but what shocks me is seeing Mr. Parker's car there too. They're clearly working together, and that makes me wonder if he hired the little asshole to hurt his own daughter.

"Are you going to tell me what happened at the hospital?" I question before we exit the car. Oliver's gaze lands on me. I know he's hiding something. It's clear as day in his gray eyes. The silver glinting at secrets.

I hate fucking secrets.

"Let's go inside," he says, ignoring my question.

Shoving the door open, I glare at him as we stalk toward the entrance. "If something happens to her . . ." I allow my words to trail off because I don't think he'll like what I have to say.

Before we have time to knock on the door, it flies open, and a man is racing toward me. The old fucker who's been using his status rears back, but before his fist makes contact, I grip his wrist, spinning him on his heels. His arm twists around behind his back.

"If you ever, come at me like that again," I hiss in his ear, "I won't think twice about ending you." It's a warning.

"You fucking savage," he bites out angrily. "My daughter is—"

"I think you'd be interested to learn my team's findings," Oliver tells him, stilling him for a moment, and I shove him away from me. The scene before me is of a man who has no fucking idea who's actually hurt Madison.

"What are you talking about?" he questions. His angry glare penetrating through Oliver, who offers him a smirk.

The cool and calm Oliver doesn't look fazed as he hands Magnus a manila folder. He steps closer, his expression deadly serious. "Why don't you have a look at the results? There were fingerprints on the blade your daughter used."

Magnus wrenches the folder open. He scans the documents, the paperwork that confirms the asshole who hurt Madison is Hudson, the man he trusted to marry her.

"Hudson?" he murmurs, shock evident in his tone.

As if he's been summoned, the man who raped and broke my girlfriend, my woman, my future fucking wife, stalks out with a smirk on his face.

"O'Leary, I suppose you've heard about Madison. It's sad—" His words spill from his mouth and into my veins, and he doesn't get to finish his sentence. That's when I see red. I see blood, and nothing can stop me from mauling the asshole. I pull my knife from my sheath, lunging at the piece of trash I'm about to take out. My fist grips his shirt, tearing the material from his body.

His fist comes out, hitting my jaw with a loud crunch. Pain sears me for a moment before I spin toward him, slamming him down on the pebbled driveway. I'm straddling him, my fist making contact with his face, again and again. I feel inhuman, and when I plunge the knife into his chest, bringing it up to his jaw, blood spurts from the cavity I've opened.

"This is for Madison," I bite out with venom dripping from my tone.

Wrath.

Revenge.

Vengeance.

Hands are on me, and I don't think when I pull the gun from my holster, aim and pull the trigger. The man behind me, Magnus Parker, falls to the ground, and Oliver's movement is automatic.

"Callan, get in my car, drive to my apartment, and

wait there for me." His order is cool and collected, as anger simmers through me. "Now."

I don't argue. I don't care about the man I shot. The asshole who's in front of me is my focus. Security guards are at the scene, and my hands are drenched in crimson. I'm drowning in the blood of my enemy, just like old times.

I grab Oliver's keys and slide into the driver's seat of his Maserati. I take one last look at the scene on the driveway, knowing Oliver is going to sort it out. He's going to do something to ensure I'm not sent to prison.

I don't know what. But I'm thankful for him.

When my gaze lifts to the doorway, I see her. A ghost of the woman I love.

She's not dead?

I blink quickly, but when I open my eyes again, she's gone.

That's what Hudson came out to tell us.

Madison Parker is dead.

And when the thought sinks in, I feel the agony of a million knives being plunged into my chest. And for the first time in my life . . . I cry.

TWENTY-SIX

CALLAN

It's been a week, seven long days of agony.

There's nothing more for me here. I should walk away.

But I can't find it in my heart to leave.

A knock at the door jerks my attention to it. Cayleigh is gone with Oliver, and Rick is with Peyton, so whoever is at the goddamn door can turn around and leave me to revel in my misery.

Another sound at the door has me growling in frustration.

"Nobody's fucking home," I grunt out, loud enough for them to hear, but instead of leaving, another harsh knock comes in response. Shoving off the sofa, I stalk toward the wooden door and grip the handle so hard I'm sure it's going to come off.

When I wrench the door wide, I'm met with deep cinnamon-colored eyes that peer up at me. Those same beautiful orbs that have pierced the cold, hard exterior of Callan O'Leary. We don't speak. The air is heavy with anxiety. Her body, those sweet supple curves tremble under my scrutiny, and I wonder if I'm dreaming. If this is some sick joke.

"Hi," she says. Even though this woman has fought a war beside me, she's fallen into her shell. A shy, timid girl stands in her place, and I almost don't recognize her.

"Blossom," I say, my voice laced with confusion. There's nothing more I want than to pull her into my arms, but I don't. Instead, I watch her shuffle her feet on the welcome mat sitting at my door.

I step aside, gesturing for her to enter my apartment. The same place I've dreamed of us sharing, of times that never happened, but in the past few days, I've pictured every moment I ever wanted with her beside me. She moves into the living room where I've fantasized about making out on the sofa with her like teenagers.

I cast a quick glance at the kitchen just beyond

where I would love to devour her sweet pussy on the countertop, along with the bedroom, where I woke up each morning thinking she was dead wishing she was beside me making my life complete.

"What are you doing here? I thought . . . I mean . . ." I stutter, turning to face her as I shut the door. Her perfume fills my nostrils, and I inhale it like a man who's been deprived of pleasure. She settles her ass on my sofa, lifting her gaze to meet mine.

"I'm not . . ." Her words trail into silence because she knows what I thought. Her father made an announcement that he needs time to grieve. We all jumped to conclusions. "I'm healed." Her whisper hanging between us like the night I said goodbye.

"I thought you died," I bite out, frustration evident in my voice. My tone is rigid with confusion, anger, need.

"I needed time," she says sullenly. "I've been living in a small apartment on the other side of town. Time has been my only friend, allowing me to think about what we've been through." All her words slowly seep into the cracks she left behind. Into the dark recesses of my mind.

"I fucking killed for you. Because I thought he

murdered you," I respond, but my voice is nowhere near as calm as I need it to be.

Each night, I went to bed seeing her face, imagining her beside me. And every morning, I woke up alone, cold, and angry at the world.

"I know why you did it," she tells me finally.

"He needed to pay." The words are gritted through my clenched teeth. Even though I'm not angry at her, and I can't blame her for her father's actions, I can hold a grudge.

"It's been a long time since I've really cared about someone so much that they become my world. The only thing I want and need. I've never loved a man before." She rises, taking tentative steps toward me. "I broke. I did fall off the wagon as they say, but I never tried to kill myself, Callan. I realized with the week I've had to recoup that the more I am away from you, the more I'm punishing myself because I fell for you."

"You came here to tell me you loved me?" At that, I tip my head to the side, regarding her through narrowed eyes.

"I came here to tell you I do love you. I still do. All

the time we spent apart was difficult. I worked through anger, frustration, and sadness. Epic fucking sadness, Callan." Her voice hardens, her words louder as she forces home the point.

"It took you a week to come to me?" She doesn't move. Her body is rigid as she lowers her gaze to the floor. I want her eyes on me. To see me. To look me in the eye and tell me what the fuck she was thinking, leaving me to think she was dead.

"I needed time," she tells me again, "because I loved you too much. I needed you to survive. My cutting was my broken part. I didn't want you to be my savior. I wanted you to be my equal. You healed me, but I realized, I needed to heal myself first because I wanted to be whole for you."

"You don't need to change who you are for me."

"I needed to change for me, Callan," she says as she moves in front of me, and my eyes eat her up like I've been starving for far too long. Madison faces me then. Her gaze lands on me, and she watches me. "I'm only myself when I'm with you. I'm stronger, but I'm still in love with you."

She's in front of me, and my hands itch to touch her. To take her and pin her against the wall, drop to my knees, and show her just how much I've missed her, but this is going to take time. There's nothing about her being here that I can rush.

"I want to be here," she tells me confidently this time.

"And the next time you see me lose my shit?"

"The next time, you won't shoot my father in the chest." Her response is sharp, honest, and raw with emotion.

Nodding, I stalk by her, trying to put distance between us, because if I don't move, I'll do something stupid. "I'm no longer in that life, Madison. I've spoken to my father," I tell her as I sit on the burgundy leather armchair. Madison returns to the sofa facing me.

"You can just walk out?" She seems as shocked as I was when I told him.

"I'll still work as security on certain jobs, but I'm no longer the man they go to for permanent fixes." She flinches at the words, but it's the only way I can say it without her running for the door. That's the last thing I want and need right now.

She nods slowly, and I know I can't fight this anymore. Rising, I settle on the sofa beside her. I can tell she's still wary, but she doesn't pull away. I can't not be near her any longer; we've been apart too long as it is. I can't fight this anymore. I turn to her, meeting those beautiful eyes that remind me of home and happiness.

"I've never loved a woman. Never loved anyone who wasn't an O'Leary. There wasn't enough in my heart to offer that to anyone. And for some reason, it never fazed me. I didn't miss it, need it, or want it," I tell her. There are tears glinting in her cinnamon eyes. They sparkle. Like the sunlight streaming through drops of honey.

She wants to look away, turning her head, but I stop her. I finally touch her after seven long days of no contact. I haven't been with another woman. I haven't even looked at another fucking woman. They didn't do anything for me. I drank, I slept, and I worked for my brother. Nothing else mattered.

"Then you walked into that fucking club," I continue. "And you knocked me on my ass."

"*Stubborn ass,*" she corrects me, and I chuckle.

"Yes, that. But honestly, Madison." I take her shaking hands in mine, lowering to the floor at her feet. I beg her for forgiveness, for salvation, and for the love she so clearly wants to offer me. "You're the only woman who's ever made me care, that's made me need and want, and the only person in this world who's offered me all that in return without asking for more."

I'm practically in her lap when I look up at her then. I can't not look into her eyes when I tell her this. Her lips are parted, and I want to claim them. I want to steal her breaths, own her moans, and revel in the taste of her sweetness.

"I love you. I have since the moment I laid my eyes on you, till the moment you walked out my door." I lean in, pressing my lips to hers, needing to make a connection, just one. Only that one kiss, and my body is alight. My heart seems to thud into action. Life flows through my veins, and I'm rabid. I need her like I need my next fucking breath.

She's everything.

She's all I want.

The love I feel when our tongues duel together in a dance meant for bed is my drug, and I shoot up as I relish her flavor. I lean in farther, needing so much more, but also needing less at the same time. I'll overdose, and it will be her that kills me.

I pull away, meeting her glittering eyes. They're like gems, shining with want.

"Callan, I came back for you," she offers in a soft whisper. Her plump lips shimmer with gloss, and they're swollen from the kiss. My mind is far off-track when I finally settle back on the sofa and pull her onto my lap.

She easily straddles me, as if she was made to be there. And I believe she was. I know without a doubt this woman is mine.

"And I've been waiting," I inform her, twirling a dark lock of her hair around my finger. "You've taken so long." My words are a slight whisper, raspy and filled with desire.

"Well, I'm here now." She lowers her body over mine, cocooning herself in my arms. "My dad is in prison. How did you not get caught after what you did to Hudson?"

"Let's just say that Oliver has connections. His team found Hudson's fingerprints on the blade that hurt you. We proved that he was the one who attempted to take your life, and he got me off on a technicality that I was protecting myself."

"His father, Gregory, has also been taken in." I nod, because that I know. Thankfully the arsehole was implicated along with Magnus. "Everything I've ever known is gone. You're the only thing that's still here. A constant." Her voice is so soft, but it's filled with love and affection. And I realize just how much I missed her.

"I'll always be here for you, Blossom," I tell her.

And that's a promise I intend to fucking keep.

TWENTY-SEVEN

MADISON

Six months later

I spent time away from Callan thinking it was what I wanted. Granted, I did need time to think, to clear my mind, but deep down, I knew in my heart he was what I needed.

When I finally woke up alone in the hospital, the first person I saw was Oliver. My father had been arrested, taken into custody. I asked after Callan, but for some reason, Oliver knew that I needed much more than Callan at the time.

He told me what happened. Everything that played out while I was unconscious. Hearing Callan had shot my father, and gutted Hudson shocked me. I knew what he did was bad, things in his past, but nothing prepared me for hearing what he'd done. But when Oliver explained the circumstances, when he'd talked to me for hours about the revelations of my father, Amber, and how she believed that she could have everything I did by sleeping her way through all the men in my life, I knew it was time I cleaned myself up, and made a choice to live, or spend forever in therapy.

Learning that my father was fucking my best friend, I felt sick to my stomach that she could do something like that. All because him, along with Gregory, and Hudson draped her in diamonds and promised her the world. Oliver though, he knew my father was using his position in the senate to do unsavory things, and Gregory wanted to overthrow him.

Gregory's thugs didn't come near me again, thankfully, and it was because of Callan following me around everywhere I went. His presence protected and kept me safe, and deep down I knew he did. Even when he wasn't there, I knew he was watching over me.

I could feel him.

My father was arrested after the video of him and

Gregory was leaked. It was all over the media. Not to mention his confession that Callan had stabbed Hudson out of self-defense shocked me. I didn't think he would testify to that, and when I asked him why he'd tell the jury that, he told me it was because he wanted me to have a happy life.

"You've always been a daughter I could be proud of. Me, on the other hand, I allowed power to take over, and I messed up. Big time. Gregory knew it and extorted it."

I watch my father through the glass. He's older, with more wrinkles than ever before. I was angry at first, but now when I look at him, I pity him.

"I want you to move on with your life. Change your name, leave the city, do whatever you want, Madison. You're my special girl."

"You confessed that Callan did it out of self defense because you felt guilty?" My tone is curious, but there's anger so clear in it too.

"I confessed because I realized something when I watched Callan kill for you. He loves you more than I ever did. And for that, I respect him." His words leave me in shock.

"Gregory had his thug threaten me because he wanted your seat on the senate?"

He nods in response. "And because Callan had given Oliver the documents first, he was scared to come after me."

Everything falls into place. I waited for the man to return. To ask me for the information, but he never came. He never contacted me again. I brushed it off. Ignored it. Now that my father is offering up everything, I realize that Callan had kept me safe even when he didn't know he was.

"Madison." My father's dark eyes meet mine. "I should've been a better parent."

"Yes, you should have. But it's in the past now."

He nods sadly, but he doesn't cry. He doesn't show any more emotion. "You better leave. I don't want you coming back here. Look forward."

And I walked out. I didn't look back.

Now that I'm home, with Callan in his apartment, I know I'm exactly where I should be. The wedding is coming up soon, and all I have to focus on is the catering and table settings. Even though it's not a big wedding, I want it to be perfect.

"Hey, sis." Peyton's sweet voice comes from the doorway.

"Peyton." I rise, giving her a hug. She's pregnant, and her belly is huge. When they found out they were having twins, Callan vowed to be the best uncle to them, and I know soon, he'll be the best father too.

"Have you chosen the place settings yet?" She smiles as I help her to the large armchair in the corner of the office.

"Not yet, but Callan wants the black and orange color scheme I told you about." I sigh, flopping in the seat beside her.

Her laugh is musical as she looks at the two options we'd narrowed it down to. There's a beautiful off-white with a citrus theme that is perfect. But, they're all pastel colors, and my amazing fiancé is not sold on them.

"Why don't you compromise, take the black out of this one" — she points her manicured finger — "and add the orange to this one?"

"And this is why I leave everything to you," I tell her.

She shrugs. "I live with one O'Leary. I know how

to get my way."

"Teach me," I beg, and she snickers at me.

"Always."

I've finally got a family. A home filled with love. And soon, I'll have my husband and our babies who I know will fill my life with everything I'd missed growing up.

EPILOGUE

CALLAN

Six months later

She's silently working on her article. I watch her tap away at the keyboard as if I'm a man hooked. I am. I was the moment I laid eyes on her. Her fire drew me to her, like a moth ready to die against the flame.

It wasn't what I felt for her at the time. It was what I didn't feel for another woman, but her. She stretches, raising her hands above her head, her head falling back, offering me a sweet glimpse of smooth skin. Her tits perk up, her lips pout, and everything I was working on flies out the goddamn window.

"Are you going to stare at me all day?" she quips, sitting back in her leather chair.

I don't respond, merely offer her a smirk. She rises, padding toward me barefoot, and I can't help reveling in her stomach swollen with my baby.

"You know, Mr. O'Leary, acting like a peeping tom is bad," she coos, straddling my lap, and I drop the notebook I'd been jotting things in to the side. Her slim thighs on either side of me, opening her up to my touch.

"I thought you liked when I was creepy?" I ask, looking up at her. Once again, I allow her to be in control. As much as I love taking over in the bedroom, there's something wickedly naughty about my woman when she takes what she needs from me.

"Mmm." She ponders my words. "Perhaps I do." Her response is grinned. Her eyes sparkle with mischief when she rolls her hips, her core pressing against my hardening cock. "Is that a knife in your pocket, or are you just glad to see me?" she quips, and I land a harsh swat on her ass.

"Don't be sassy, Blossom. I'm not averse to spanking my pregnant wife," I tell her honestly, because fuck I'd love to see her caramel flesh glow bright red with my handprint.

"Didn't you already claim me? I mean, your baby will be coming out of me in"— she glances at the clock on the desk — "three months."

"I know, but you're so pretty when you cry, Blossom," I tell her, pulling her in for a kiss on those plump lips I love watching swallow my dick.

"You're insatiable," she admonishes with a smile on her pretty face.

"Can you two stop fucking for two minutes?" Carrick stalks into the study where Madison is still perched on my lap. His blonde beauty follows behind him.

"Oh please," Peyton responds. "You do realize you're just as bad as he is?"

He rolls his eyes, unbuttoning his suit jacket as he settles himself in the armchair. "I'm having a party this weekend for Erin and Fallon," he informs me and Madison.

"They'll be three months old, and we'd like to have a party. That is, of course, if your little one doesn't arrive early." Peyton smiles, her big, green eyes sparkling with excitement.

My brother and his wife have twin girls, and they both have their daddy wrapped around their little fingers.

"Sounds good," I respond. "Who else is coming?"

"Mason and Savvie will be there, along with their aunt Cayleigh. I've just spoken to Nate and Eva. They'll bring their little boy, Ainsley. And then we're waiting on Elijah and Gia to let us know if they're able to come. Gia's just had a baby, a little girl they've named Raquel," Peyton informs me. "Oh! And Chance, my brother, will be there, too, with Oliver."

"We'll be there definitely."

"Great, a family get-together," Carrick smirks.

This is life. I watch my brother with Peyton, and I am thankful to a God I no longer believe in that we're still here. Our lives have moved on, we've found love, and we've finally stepped out from under the family obligations that held us back for so long.

When my father learned that I wanted to live in America, he wasn't angry. I thought he'd disown us both, but he understood. There are times I wonder what it would be like to go back to that life, but now, with my new job running my own security company, I'm happy.

As I sit with my brother, sister in-law, and my wife, who's still straddling my lap, I find I truly am content with my life. Only ruthless now in pleasuring my Blossom. And looking forward to spoiling the fa

PLAYLIST

- Begging for Thread - Banks
- Two Weeks - FKA Twigs
- Monsters - Ruelle
- Madness - Ruelle
- Dirty Mind - Boy Epic
- All the King's Men - The Rigs
- Devil's Playground - The Rigs
- Desire - Meg Myers
- Take Me to Church - MILCK
- River - Bishop Briggs
- Him & I - G-Eazy, Halsey
- Numb - Linkin Park
- Bleed It Out - Linkin Park
- Ghost Magnetic - David Cook
- Save Yourself - Birdy
- Whispers in the Dark - Skillet

ACKNOWLEDGMENTS

Writing this book was difficult, not because of the storyline or the characters, but because I wanted to make sure that I portrayed Madison's pain accurately. I wanted to make sure that as much as you love someone, they can never 'fix' you, 'change' you, and you shouldn't allow them to. Focus on yourself before leaning on someone. Love yourself, and that is when someone will love you. Callan and Madison's journey are extremely personal to me, and for me to be able to share it with you, the reader, I'm deeply humbled.

Firstly, I need to thank my partner in life. He's stood by me through every journey I've been on, he's offered me advice, love, and support, and most of all, he puts up with my crazy (and trust me, there's a lot of crazy to keep calm).

To my ALPHA reader on this story, Allyson, you have been one heck of a rock for me. You've taken this story and given me your honest, brutal feedback, and I'm so thankful to have worked with you on this, (and the future projects I have coming up).

My BETAs—Cat, Melissa, Joy, Sheena, Caroline, Amy, and Lisa thank you for being there for me and reading the rough drafts of my words. Your encouragement and never-ending support are the foundation behind my books.

Candy, you know I love your crazy! Thank you for editing and polishing Callan and for loving him so much! :P He'll leave his knife at home and take you out for dinner some time. And who knows, there may be some glistening too!

My Angels street team—Tre, Sheena, Sarah, Lisa, Caroline, TJ, Hayfaah, Joy, Cinders, Christiann, Fran, Erin, Pam, Tanya, Kim—thank you for pimping my work EVERYWHERE. You ladies rock!!

My reader group, The Darklings, as always, you're the only place I know I'll find like-minded ladies and a handful of gents who will have a laugh without drama. The group has grown so much and I'm excited for the future! Thank you for being there.

To all my author colleagues, thank you for always sharing, commenting, and supporting me. I appreciate every one of you. Having a support system is important and you ladies provide that and so much more.

Readers and bloggers, from the bottom of my little black heart, THANK YOU. All you do for us authors is incredible. Reading and reviewing is demanding on your own time and you do it with a smile. Thank you so, so much. You are valued and appreciated for taking time out to show us so much love.

If you enjoyed this story, please consider leaving a review. I'd love you forever. (Even though I already do!)

SINS OF SEVEN

ABOUT DANI

Dani is a USA Today Bestselling Author of dark and deviant romance with a seductive edge.

Originally from Cape Town, South Africa, she now lives in the UK with her better half who does all the cooking while she writes all the words.

When she's not writing, she can be found binge-watching the latest TV series, or working on graphic design either for herself, or other indie authors. She enjoys reading books about handsome villains and feisty heroines, mostly dark, always seductive, and sometimes depraved.

She has a healthy addiction to tattoos, coffee, and ice cream.

www.danirene.com

info@danirene.com

FIND DANI ONLINE

Do you follow me?

If not, head over to any of the below links,

I love to hear from my readers!

Amazon - http://bit.ly/DaniAmazon

BookBub - http://bit.ly/DaniBookBub

Facebook - http://bit.ly/DaniFBPage

Facebook Group - Dani's Deviants

Goodreads - http://bit.ly/DaniGoodreads

Twitter - @danireneauthor

Pinterest - @danireneauthor

Instagram - @danireneauthor

Spotify - http://bit.ly/DaniSpotify

OTHER BOOKS